Tight Knit

ALLIE BRENNAN

DEDICATION

Te iubesc cu toata inima, Nana ~ I love you with all my
heart, Nana

CONTENTS

ACKNOWLEDGMENTS

This book wouldn't have happened without the support and encouragement from those close to me, and even some far away. Thanks to Travis for being my 'bad boy'. Thanks to my wordsprint partner, Courtney, for keeping me on track and making sure I stuck to my word count. Thanks to my readers: Ainslie, Olivia, Nyrae, Jolene and Leigh. A big thanks to my brutal editor, but loving mother, Darlene

CHAPTER ONE
Talia

The tips of my fingers tingle with frantic energy. I snap my wrist to try and expel the building anxiety that so often grips me. I lean back against the warm bricks of the mini-mall and dig my toe into a crack in the sidewalk.

Just calm down, I tell myself, pulling my cell phone away from my ear. I really don't feel any better about this and talking to Deacon isn't helping.

Taking a deep breath I concentrate on my beating heart. This really shouldn't be such a big deal. It's just a knitting club meeting.

Another breath. It's okay that I'm alone. Nan just isn't feeling well. She'll be back next week. That's what she said.

"I just need a break, darling. I think I'm coming down with something," her words echo through my head.

It's not the words that concerned me. It was how she wouldn't look at me when she said them.

A muffled sound catches my attention and I remember I'm still holding my cell phone away from my ear.

"Talia, are you listening to me?" Deacon's voice comes through the speaker.

"Yeah, yeah, I'm here." I tilt the phone so he can't hear my breathing.

A sharp pain shoots through my chest and I press my hand hard against the spot that hurts. I hate this feeling. It's moments like this I wish I was still on meds. Moments when I *want* to be numb so I don't have to face this never-ending doom.

"Are you freaking out?" Deacon asks, because he can't actually call them what they are. A panic attack. It's not hard to say, but for him it is, I guess. Even after two months.

"I'm fine." I lie. I do that a lot now. Lie to Deacon.

"It's just a knitting club meeting. It's not like you were elected president." He is on edge. Distracted. This isn't like him.

Yeah, actually I was, I think. Stepping in as

president of the Tight Knit Society for one
week would probably mean nothing to
anyone else, but for me it might as well be
the end of the world. I work hard to stay
unnoticed. Leadership roles equal disaster
for me.

I struggle to push back the thick layer of
negative thoughts that are always waiting to
blanket my mind with darkness.

"Yeah," I mumble and shift position, still
vibrating with energy. I hear a familiar voice
in the background. "Are you with Janna?" I
ask.

Good. I need to change the subject. I have
no idea why I'm so freaked out by this
meeting.

"Yeah, why?" he says sharply, which
startles me and I stand up straighter.

"I'm supposed to meet her later." The
swirling mess in my mind sinks down my
spine and settles in my stomach. Something
doesn't feel right.

"Just come over to my place, we'll be
around." He hangs up without saying
goodbye, which is not like Deacon either, but
I don't have time to dissect my boyfriend's
increasingly odd behavior.

Man, I wish Nan were here.

I slide my cellphone shut and push off the
brick wall. I take one more deep breath

before stepping up to the door of Nan's favorite wool shop. The bell jingles softly and the familiar warmth of Tight Knit Wool and Accessories envelops me, making me forget Deacon. The shop smells like Nan. Like soap and baking and freshly spun wool.

My shoulders slump forward for only a second before I'm jabbed in the spine.

"You stand up straight, Talia, or you'll end up like Georgina, all snake spine-ed, when you're old," says the crackly voice of The Tight Knit Society's resident know-it-all, Marybeth. I can't stop myself from smiling. It's amazing how stereotypical The Tight Knitters are sometimes. I make my way to the circle of couches in the center of the store while fishing a container of Pecan cookies from the bag slung over my shoulder.

"Oh, you're a damn liar, Marybeth. You know full well it's the osteoporosis that curved my back," Georgina glances up at us from her regular spot on the couch and I smile. Her eyes are a watery blue and her white hair shines in the warm light. Her face is all kindness and a lifetime of experience. Georgina is the oldest in our group and I am the youngest; it's something we bond over.

Marybeth coughs, a deep chronic-smokers cough, and waves her hand at Georgina dismissively. Marybeth's signature bright red fingernails contrast with her thinning pale skin, an her silvery hair is pulled back off her face. She looks down at my cookies with narrowed eyes. She knows Nan didn't make them.

"You haven't even tried one yet, stop criticizing me," I scowl at her and curl the container into my chest. She looks like I had said I baked them in the nude, but she isn't shocked; she just loves drama.

"You don't let that Marybeth give you a hard time, Talia. She's had a hard life but you tell her to mind her own business when you need to." I hear Nan say.

I lift my fabric shoulder bag over my head and set it down next to my spot. Riffling through the mess of yarn in my bag, I pull out my leather case of needles and a hat that I had just finished the night before. I smooth the soft black wool out running a finger over the slanted cable that braids its way around the hat from the top to bottom in a spiral pattern.

Marybeth snatches it right out of my hands and a pulse of nervous energy surges through me leaving dizziness in its wake. How did I not know she would be the first? She stretches the hat out then puts her hand inside, feeling the knits and purls, inspecting the cable by putting it up to the tip of her nose.

"What's this?" Her dark eyes never leave the hat.

"It's a hat," I say. I sit down hard in my chair. My heart still hasn't fully recovered from talking to Deacon and I'm exhausted from trying to keep the panic out.

How does she not know it's a hat?

"It looks like a giant's sock," Marybeth passes the hat to Georgina who places the sock-hat onto her head and pulls it right down to her chin before the top of the hat touches the crown of her head.

Anna, the next youngest Knitter at 40-something, looks over her glasses and smiles sympathetically. She's a high school teacher. She gets it.

"I don't see how this is helpful?" Georgina's shaky voice is muffled by the wool.

I laugh despite my mood and move over to her, leaning on the arm of the old couch. I pull the hat up.

"It's a slouch hat, or a beanie some people call them," I explain, readjusting the hat on Georgina so wisps of her short white hair stick out around her face and the excess material slouches down to her neck.

"It doesn't even completely cover my ears this way," Georgina pulls the hat down around her ears and the excess wool stands straight up. Everyone laughs this time and I yank the hat from her head and put it on my own. I tuck the back half of my dark hair into the hat and let two big layered chunks of hair hang around my face to accompany my bangs.

"It's not really supposed to cover your ears. It's just for looks."

I am met by six pairs of blank eyes.

Anna just smiles to herself and shakes her head, keeping her eyes on her work, never breaking the rhythm of her clacking needles. I sigh and unroll my own knitting needles.

Trying to introduce something new to a group of old ladies is like trying to untangle a knotted ball of yarn.

"Start at the beginning and go slowly, yard by yard, and eventually you'll get to the end. If you try to go too fast, you'll just make it worse." Nan told me when I first started with the Knitters and wanted to make gloves with no fingers. It was as if I said the Holocaust didn't happen with the fuss they kicked up over it.

Anna pours me a cup of lavender tea, and all the ladies commend me on my cookies, even though I know they all think Nan's are better. Which they are.

I feel lost here without Nan. She's my safe

place and without her I'm exposed. I don't have my wall of strength but the knitting helps keep the panic away. It's why I joined the club in the first place. So I focus on the knitting. I cast on and start to make a new hat.

Georgina hums the same tune she does every week. She has the most beautiful voice. The soft vibration of her humming, along with the clicking needles and the odd slurp of tea and shifting of position, helps to ease my nerves. Next to Nan, Georgina is the only other Knitter I have been able to truly connect with. I always mean to ask her what song it is, but never want to interrupt.

"So my grandson is picking me up today," Georgina says throwing a glance my way. "But he's going to be a bit late so I'm just going to knit until he gets here."

I scrunch up my nose. Why is she looking at me like that? No one cares if she stays late or leaves early, especially me.

I've heard tons of stories about 'her Lannie', but I never met him, so I am unsure why her eyes are narrowed specifically at me.

But I've seen this expression before.

I see Marybeth watching me, too. She's waiting for something.

Here's the catch.

"Talia, I'd like it if you could stay as well. We have to discuss the charity drive since you're standing in for Florence."

My heart starts hammering in my chest. This is exactly why I didn't want to come today. Standing in. I don't want to stand in.

How did I get this job anyway? Just because I'm blood related? This isn't the monarchy. I tap my foot rapidly on the wooden floor.

"Yeah, okay. I'll stay." I try to continue knitting but my hands are shaking so bad I drop three stitches. I stop to crack my wrists and roll my shoulders before starting the row again.

Slowly each of the ladies begins packing up their things and leaving. For the most part this is just like any other meeting, except Nan's empty chair. Except for my rampant nerves having an epic battle inside me.

She'll be back next week, I think, *Just get through today and she'll be back next week.*

~

Everyone is gone except for Georgina and me. I sit in Nan's chair leaning back to let my body sink into the cushions, just like I sink into her warm hugs. It helps. A little.

Georgina moves to sit beside me and takes my hand in hers like only a grandmother can. The shaking slows.

"We have to start planning the Christmas Charity Drive, dear. Florence always plans it, but if she can't see her way to do it this year, I know for absolute certainty no one else will.

I stare at her.

"She'll be back next week," I say, unconvincingly, as I remember the way Nan averted her eyes when she told me it was 'just a bug'.

"Yes, yes," Georgina pats my hand, "But if she can't do it, Talia, we are the only ones. You and me."

Any control I may have gained over the shaking is gone. My hand vibrates inside Georgina's.

"But..." I can't get past that look in Georgina's eyes. It's like Nan's was. Like she knows more than she's telling me.

"But this event is the most important event of the year to your Nan. I think we owe it to her to help make it the best yet."

The annual Cozy Christmas Charity Drive is the Tight Knit Society's only event. The Drive is the city's biggest art and craft sale. It's huge. Nan always blows everyone else out of the water with her booth designs and sales records.

I grip the hem of my sweater. I feel the thoughts start to creep in from the edges of my mind. A surge of energy forces me to shift in my seat. I chew on my index finger.

If I plan the show it means I'll have to work with the Director, who happens to be Greta Finnley, Deacon's grandma. I can't commit to that. Mostly because I'm not sure I'm committed to Deacon. No. That would be a nightmare. What if Deacon and I broke up?

There has to be someone else.

"But what about Anna?" I protest.

My heart speeds up. I do not want to do this.

"She works full time and has a family to take care of. Her boy has Autism. You know that, Talia."

"Right, sorry. How about Marybeth?" I smile right after I say it, unable to hold in a laugh. It settles the nerves crackling under my skin for just a second.

"Do you want Marybeth to help plan the Drive?"

"No, no you're right. But school starts this week and I'll be busy."

"With what, dear? Are you in drama? Playing on the varsity basketball team? A mathlete?" She chuckles to herself as I shake my head to every one. She knows I'm the biggest social outcast at school. She knows I make myself invisible by choice. My hand drops from my mouth, and I pull at the hem of my sweater with more force now. I can't do this. I'd have to talk to people. I'd have a panic attack a day. The Drive would be a disaster.

"I can help with anything that needs to be done inside your school hours." Georgina continues, "and my Lannie can help with any set up or lifting."

Georgina seems proud of herself.

Thanks. Thanks for setting off a panic attack.

I nervously adjust the hat on my head and pull headphones out of my bag, wrapping them around my neck. Music drowns out the thoughts. There are definitely too many thoughts right now.

I fidget and want to slide the headphones over my ears and just pretend I'm not having this conversation. As if I can plan an event this huge if I can't even handle talking about it.

"I'll think about it." I already thought about it. No.

"But Talia..."

"I need to talk to Nan first."

Georgina opens her mouth to speak but is cut off by the jingling of the door. A guy around my age ducks slightly as he walks through the door and scans the room. I only have to see his profile to recognize him.

His dark eyes take in everything with an

intensity that forces me to shift uncomfortably in my seat. It's as if he's memorizing every inch of the store. His thick eyebrows are pulled down low. He looks angry.

He always looks angry.

Everyone around here knows Lachlan McCreedy. He is the most dangerous guy at school and his life is as legendary as it is secretive.

His black curls hang haphazardly like he hasn't brushed them once in his life and he nods his head to move the strands from his pale, angular face.

What really makes Lachlan recognizable are the tattoos spiraling down his right arm from his T-shirt to his wristband and continuing onto the back of his hand. From this distance they're nothing but a burst of colour and shape. I've always wanted to know what they were, but never had the nerve to get close enough to see.

I'm wondering why he would ever be in this place when his glare finds us. His eyes briefly pass over me, lingering for only a second, and then his face softens when he looks at Georgina.

Lachlan... lan... Lannie...

Lachlan *can't* be Georgina's grandson

CHAPTER TWO

Lachlan

Gram is never late. When I drive her, which is almost never, she's always waiting on the sidewalk but today the sidewalk in front of the small row of shops is empty.

At first I am annoyed, but as the minutes pass I start to get worried. No one goes into or out of the shop for about 15 minutes. The worry turns into irritated concern. I cut the engine to Gram's old four-door sedan and get out, slamming the door a little harder than I need to.

I push through the front door of the Wool Shop. It smells of old ladies and dust. I scan the store, which is pretty much empty until I see her.

Gram's sitting on a couch in the middle of the store next to a girl who looks like she wants to disappear into the chair she's in.

The girl is watching me with big dark blue eyes. Her chocolate colored bangs cut straight across her forehead covering her raised eyebrows. She has that wide doe-eyed fear that tells me she recognizes me, but I have no idea who she is. Not the type of girl I'd remember.

I look at Gram. She has a huge smile on her face. The one that makes her eyes dance with life. It's my favorite one. Not that I ever tell her.

"Gram," I swing my arms out then shove them into the pockets of my jeans. "I've been waiting. Where the hell–"

Gram stands up, letting go of the girl's small hand. She narrows her eyes and my mouth snaps shut.

"Lannie! You watch your mouth, son." Gram is tiny and frail but I know better than to mess with her when she has that look. I make it over to her in three steps.

"Sorry, Gram." I slide my arm around her shoulder and toss my best smile down at her. It works pretty much every time. I open my mouth to tell her I was worried, but remember the girl. I know it's completely messed up but I don't want to say it in front of her. I also don't need this girl knowing I'm going to be late for the last meeting with my probation officer. I pull lightly on Gram's shoulders to try to guide her to the door but she has her feet planted and that's that. I know Gram better than to keep trying.

"I wanted you to meet someone. This is Talia Gregory." Gram looks from me to Talia and back again. She has that big grin on again but this time it's laced with a smugness that says there is more to this introduction than I think. I groan quietly and shift my weight. Her insistence that I drive her today totally makes sense now.

She's been planning this all day.

Great. I'm being set up by my grandmother with a girl in a knitting club who doesn't look a day over sixteen. Gram knows nothing about my taste in women. Or maybe she does...

"Hey," I say coolly and Talia's head lowers, shifting her gaze into her lap. The back of her hair is tucked into a wool hat. A pretty fucking awesome hat.

"Nice hat. I've been looking for one like that. Where'd you get it?" I try to ignore the fact that Gram is looking back and forth between us like a cat watching a Ping-Pong game.

Talia looks up. Her eyes are the darkest blue. I didn't even know that eye colour existed.

"I made it." Her voice is soft but high

pitched. I'm not sure if that's how she always sounds or if she is just scared of me.

Most people are just scared of me, so I'll go with the general consensus.

"How much would you charge to make another one?" I kind of want that hat. I've looked everywhere for one. But all the ones I've found are trendy and lame.

Gram reaches over and tugs the hat off Talia's head causing waves of hair to spill messily over her shoulders. Talia's shocked but she doesn't make a move for it. Her cheeks flush a light pink.

Is she shaking?

She totally looks like a deer. Completely pure and innocent. I'm wondering what that innocence would feel like, which shocks me. I don't think I've ever been innocent. Not like her. Not truly. Until this moment I don't think I've ever thought about it either.

Gram shoves the hat into my hands pulling me from my thoughts. A smell similar to Grams vanilla almond cookies fills the air around me.

"Here, you can have this one."

"Gram!" I try to give the hat back to Talia but Gram intercepts it.

"It's okay. You can have it," Talia practically whispers.

I try to protest but Gram cuts me off.

"I'll pay her for the hat. She's making a hundred more for the Christmas charity drive anyways, right, Talia?"

Talia looks from Gram to me and nods her head slowly. Her cheeks go from pink to red and she stands up with a jerky movement. She is a lot shorter than me. Her hands are shaking. This chick is seriously tense.

"I should go."

"Do you need a ride, dear?" Grams eyes sparkle and I feel sorry for Talia. I am never embarrassed by Gram, but right now, I'm bordering on it.

"No," she says sharply, her face going three shades redder, "I mean, I have my bike and I have to meet my, uh, boyfriend."

She keeps her head down as she heaves her multi-colored bag over her shoulder and fits her old-school headphones over her ears. I can tell she wants to get out of there as fast as possible. And, so do I.

~

"So, are you going to explain yourself?" I ask when we're in the car. Gram stares blankly and I raise my eyebrow.

"Explain what, son?" She shrugs and I can't help but smirk.

"You know damn well what, Gram."

"Watch your mouth."

"I'm almost 18, and damn isn't even a

swear."

"It is in my house."

"Stop changing the subject." I smile wider and shift the car into drive.

"What were we talking about?" Gram always fakes dementia when she wants to get away with something.

"You can't just force me onto girls you know, Gram. This isn't the 1800's. That girl looked terrified. And, you practically stole her hat." I rub my thumb over the wool as I speak. The dark fibers are soft and still warm. A faint scent of vanilla hangs in the air.

"I did no such thing." Her voice goes up and she clutches at her sweater dramatically.

I roll my eyes.

"Yeah, okay Gram."

"I'll pay her for the hat. I said that already. Now Lannie, I'll drop you off at your meeting, I need to pick up some things from the store. Call me when you're done."

I laugh and toss the hat over my shoulder into the back seat.

No one can compete with the stubbornness of old ladies.

~

Officer Rawlins has a small, warm office. It's inviting and has pictures of calming scenery and waterfalls and shit. Doesn't change the fact that I hate coming here. I hate the clacking sound of his keyboard as he takes notes. I hate how he looks at me with that genuine concern. Like he actually wants to help me.

He's wearing that 'concern' now. His thick greying eyebrows push together and his dark eyes set in a hard stare. I don't like when people try and look inside me like this. Wrinkles run across Rawlins forehead, but there's a small smile hidden behind his greying beard.

His hand gestures to the chair opposite him. I sit, lean back and throw my arm over the back of the chair next to me.

"Hello, Lachlan. How are you today? Excited that this is our last meeting, no doubt." He chuckles.

I thought Probation Officers were supposed to he hard asses. Jerks. Power hungry douchebags who couldn't hack it in real cop school. But Rawlins is soft spoken, rational and real. He isn't a push over but he's never made me feel like punching him either, like my previous PO. It puts me on edge.

I run my hand over my tattooed arm, my fingers bumping over all the scars. Let's just say I'm not used to guys like him.

"Yeah, I guess," I answer, and he starts clacking away on his keyboard. I crack my knuckles. I don't know why but I want nothing more than to smash that keyboard. I liked it better when he wrote it down on paper, and I learned to read upside down to see what he was saying about me.

Rawlins mumbles some stuff as he types and asks me questions in between. He doesn't waste time with niceties. I like that about him.

"You were arrested at the age of 15 on one count of drug trafficking, resisting arrest and underage drinking, is that correct?"

My heart is slamming against my ribs and my knuckles are white. I hadn't noticed that I had balled them into fists.

Why is he bringing this up again? How I ended up in this chair once a month is the last thing I want to talk about.

Why can't we just say see ya later, and get it done with?

"Yes." I spit through clenched teeth.

"And this was just three weeks after your mother's arrest?"

I nod. I don't want to talk about her either.

"You were... MIA, shall we say, for those three weeks?"

"What does this have to do with anything? Just like to relive the good times on our last meeting?" I mutter. But I wasn't MIA, I was on a three-week bender where I smoked, drank, ate, snorted and screwed everything I could. I'm not proud of it. Rawlins knows that.

Rawlins looks over his computer and I'm sure he's smiling even though I can't see the bottom of his face.

"I'm closing your file, Lachlan. You should be happy. But first we have to make sure nothing's changed. Paperwork and government. You know how these things go."

I stretch my arms up then rest them on my head. I lean further down into the chair.

Rawlins knows me well enough to read me and when I stay silent, he continues.

"Just before your 16th birthday, you were sentenced to four months in a federal juvenile detention center, six months community service and two years probation, completing your incarceration and community service on time and in good standing?"

I tilt my head toward the ceiling.

"Yeah." My leg bounces up and down, my heel slamming down on the tiled floor. I force out the memories, I'm good at keeping them at a distance. I'm good at keeping most things at a distance. Which is why I get so agitated when someone tries to dig up my expertly covered past.

"And you were given this sentencing in

part because of the circumstances leading up to your arrest and in part because your grandmother, who is an upstanding member of this community, testified under oath and took full legal and financial responsibility for you and your actions?"

My head snaps up. My heart starts hammering again but not from anger this time.

"I didn't know that," I lean forward and put my forearms on his desk. It's Rawlins turn to lean back in his chair and cross his arms, resting them on his belly.

"Well, you are turning 18 in a couple months and will officially be an adult. I think it's important for you to know. It's important for you to know how much she sacrificed for you because she believed in you. You're lucky to have her."

My jaw hinges up and down a couple times. Why didn't she ever tell me that? I thought they gave me a lighter sentence because of *him*. I run my hand along my tattoos again and lean back. The tattoos my Gram had paid for, just to help me cover up the scars. To turn them into something beautiful. Meaningful.

My fingers move along my forearm in a zig zag pattern following the lines of my favorite tattoo. The tattoo that means the most to me.

It's also the one people hate the most with torn and rotting skin being sewn back together with yarn from my wrist to my elbow, covering the hellish and horrifying imagery beneath it. To me it means the most. This is the tattoo that Gram inspired. She's the only one who can stitch me back together. She's the only one who's ever tried.

I don't know why I'm surprised that she would take full responsibility for me.

I do know I'm doing a bad job of making it up to her.

The rest of the meeting is quick. I answer yes and no to all his questions and I'm standing up to leave before I know it.

Rawlins reaches over his desk and holds out his hand. I shake it.

"Well, you take care of yourself Lachlan. I have high hopes for you."

I shove my hands in my pockets. That's his first mistake. No one should have high hopes for people like me.

"Yeah, uh, thanks. It feels good to be outta shackles." I half-smile at him. He laughs.

"Well you still have a couple more support meetings. So you're not *completely* off the hook yet."

Ah, fuck. If there's anything I hate more than probation, it's my support group.

"Yeah, I'll be there. Take it easy, Rawlins."

"Say hello to Georgina for me."

I just nod as I walk out the door.

~

"You know you spoil me, right?" I ask Gram over my steaming plate of spaghetti. My serving is three times the size of hers. She cuts her spaghetti with a knife and fork while I just scoop and slurp mine into my mouth.

"You know you eat like an Ox, right?" Gram smiles and I smile back.

"I'm a growing boy."

"Well one day you're going to stop growing up and start growing out," Gram pats her small belly and I snort.

"Do women always care about the size of their stomachs?"

"Til the day they die, son."

"Will they ever know that we don't really care?"

"Do men always think everything is about them?" She mocks.

"Til the day they die, Gram." I wink at her.

It is moments like this when I am truly happy. I can't imagine life without Gram. Actually, I can. I never want to go back there.

My phone buzzes in my pocket, vibrating against my leg. I wipe my hands on my jeans and ignore Gram's frown while I fish the cell out of my pocket.

Midnight. Last time.

The text has a happy looking speech bubble around it. There's nothing happy about this message.

"Your mother called today," Gram says absent-minded. The words jar me from my thoughts and I tuck the phone back in my pocket.

"Yeah?" I don't really want to talk about my mom.

"She wanted me to wish you luck with your Probation meeting and that she loves you very much."

I roll my eyes and Gram glares.

"She didn't want to remind me why it's my fault she's in prison this time."

"Watch your attitude, Lannie. You're not the only one in this world that's had to make difficult choices."

I hold back a laugh. Her choices were easy. She always chose him.

"Sorry, Gram." I force a smile and stand up to clear the dishes.

"You may not see it but she loves you more than you know. Someday you'll realize the sacrifices made in this family and you won't be rolling your eyes like a little boy."

Rawlins' words echo through my mind. Gram's sacrifices. The ones she made for me. Those are the only ones that mean anything to me. Not Mom's. Gram's.

The realization feels like an unexpected punch in the gut. It actually hurts.

CHAPTER THREE

Talia

I'm stopped at a red light, one foot on the curb to balance my old Beachcomber bike and one eye on the flashing red 'don't walk' sign. I have one headphone piece on my ear and the other off so I can hear the traffic. I slide my phone open and send Janna a quick text. She'll get a kick out of this. She has been boy crazy since the first day of kindergarten. My hands are still shaking a little.

You'll never guess what just happened to me...

I throw the phone in my bag. The light turns green and I continue my way to Vista Court.

I'm in shock that Georgina tried to pawn me off on her grandson but now that I've calmed down a bit it's more absurd than anything else.

Lachlan McCreedy.

On this, or any other alternate universe, us

even being friends is a ridiculous thought.

It's not like he's *the* hottest guy in school or anything, but Lachlan is a big deal. He gets noticed. He's a senior so I never see him, mostly because I make myself invisible. But everybody knows him, and everybody stays out of his way. Not shocking, considering his constant glare and those massive tattoos.

I've heard Georgina tell stories about how perfect and wonderful her grandson is for almost a year and never ever would I have made the connection that Lannie was Lachlan. Never.

It's like he has a split personality. Or Georgina is delusional. Or all the rumors about Lachlan aren't true. I don't know which one to settle on.

When I steer my bike up Deacon's driveway, Janna is waiting for me. Her long body leans up against the oversized three-car garage making her look shorter and smaller than she is. Her red hair is wet and tangled around her shoulders. I've always been envious of her. I wish I knew what that felt like to be so laid back. Janna's never stressed out about anything. I think it's why we've stayed friends for so long. I stress and she makes a joke out of it. I panic and she distracts me with something fun. I get upset and she does that thing with her voice that makes me laugh every time.

When she sees me she pushes off the garage and skips down to me straddling the front tire of my bike. I notice for the first time that she's not wearing pants.

That's a little weird, seeing as she's at my boyfriend's house. But I guess she's been friends with Deacon longer than she's been friends with me. Still, a little weird.

"Why are you looking at me like that?" She shakes my bike gently.

"Like what?" I ask but I notice my nose is wrinkled and I'm glaring at her.

"Like I just hit on your dad or something."

"You're not wearing pants."

Janna laughs. It seems so easy for her.

"Tali, I was swimming. Would you rather I go naked?"

I shake my head and smile.

"D and I used to bathe together. Totally no big deal."

We walk to the back yard and I lean my bike on the fence.

Well you didn't look like this when you were three, I think, scanning her stupidly long legs, then push the thought out of my mind. I crack my wrists. I don't need to panic right now. It's not a big deal. They're swimming. I trust her. She's my only friend and she can have any guy she wants. They've known each other their whole lives.

Deacon's in the pool and as soon as I see him I get that nauseous feeling I always get when I know something bad is going to happen. Something is wrong with us, but watching him I wonder if it was ever right with us. Janna set us up. I didn't want to do it. I'm still not sure if I'm with him for me, or her.

Janna has her arm looped through mine and she tugs me closer to the pool.

"You okay?" she laughs. "You look like you're going to barf."

I hate that I'm so transparent. I hate that I'm so afraid of everything.

Deacon looks at me, his arms crossed on the cement lip of the pool and his body floating out behind him. He has the perfect smile. Too perfect, like it's not real. I always catch myself thinking things like that. How can someone like him like someone like me? It's so stupid. There's nothing wrong with me. Well, nothing a little Valium can't handle.

"Babe," he says and I grit my teeth. "Hey, come in the water."

The sun suddenly feels a thousand times hotter but the water doesn't seem any more appealing. The beads of liquid roll down his neck and muscular chest. This is one of those him-equals-better-than-me   moments.

Suddenly, my heart pounds.

"I didn't bring a bathing suit," I say, even though Janna didn't either and that didn't stop her.

"Just go in your underwear," he says like it should be obvious. It is obvious. I just don't want to.

"No, I'm good. I'll just sit here."

My breathing's getting faster and I feel thoughts splash and shatter through my mind like the drops of water falling from Deacon's frown. I snap my wrist a couple of times to try and shake out the anxiety. It doesn't work so I sit and dip my feet in the cool water.

"Aw, come on, babe. Don't be such a prude." Deacon is sliding his hands up my legs. I pretend to adjust and pull my feet up and cross them beneath me.

"I'm not a prude." I glare at him. "I just have to go visit Nan right away and don't want to be wet."

I'm being defensive. I just don't want to.

How does that make me a prude?

Deacon rolls his eyes and disappears under the water.

Janna pats my knee.

"You want me to go with you?"

"Nah, It's okay. But I should go. Don't want to go too late, Nan might have plans."

Which is a lie. I'm with Nan every second that I'm not at home or with Janna.

I'm just really uncomfortable right now. The nervous vibration in my limbs is telling me I need to get out of here.

Is that normal? To be uncomfortable around your boyfriend? To not want to be around him?

"I'll walk out with you." Janna pulls her legs from the water.

"No, really J. I'm fine. You stay." I smile and hug her with one arm while fishing my headphones out of my bag with the other.

"Okay, but call me later. You didn't tell me what you meant by that text."

I had totally forgotten about that.

I waved to Deacon and forced my shaking body to leave the backyard.

Today is a bad day. Some days I can handle the nerves, but I never know when they'll go haywire. When they do, there's nothing I can do about it. I need to get to Nan.

I'm almost to my bike when a strong hand grips my shoulder and I stop walking. Deacon slides his other hand around my waist and pulls me into him.

"Where are you going?" He kisses my neck and my body goes cold.

This isn't right. It should be the opposite. His touch should heat me up.

When we first started dating I wanted him to kiss me, to touch me. What's happened?

I swivel my body so I'm facing him and he squeezes me tighter.

"I've gotta go, Deacon." My voice shakes. I put my hands on his chest and push lightly but he doesn't let me go.

"You spend too much time with your grandma, Tal. It's kind of lame. Stay here. My parents are gone. There's lots of stuff we can do that's way more fun." His hands slip under my sweater and he squeezes my hips. I shake harder.

I push harder, he pulls harder. My breath comes in quick bursts. My vision blurs and waves of energy crash around my brain.

Let me go, I think but I can't say it. He's my boyfriend but I don't want him to touch me. It's not right. My body spasms. I can't stop it.

Deacon lets me go and I stumble backwards into the garage, sliding down the vinyl paneling. I hadn't realized I was pushing him so hard.

"Seriously? Are you seriously freaking out right now?" Deacon glares down at me. "Am I not allowed to touch my girlfriend?"

I shift my eyes away from him and stay silent. After a few seconds I hear him walk away and the gate slams.

He doesn't get it.

~

I ride my bike toward Nan's house in a trance. My stomach is still churning and my thoughts keep skimming the edges of panic over how he wouldn't let me go, how Janna was in her underwear, how I felt like someone stuck ice in my shirt when he touched me. *Just forget it,* I think, *Guys are jerks. And perverts. It's no big deal.*

I press my feet to the pedals hard and ride as fast as I can. The air is cooling fast and I'm shivering by the time I get to Nan's. I throw my bike on the grass and take the porch steps two at a time. I know Nan's house better than my own. Kicking my flip flops off in the entryway, I walk straight through the kitchen to the living room.

Nan's sitting on the couch, her knees pulled up and her long arms wrapped around them. She is the tallest, slenderest lady I've ever known. I definitely didn't get that from her. I'm short and no one would describe me as slender. More like Georgina. Soft.

A smile spreads across her face when she sees me. She usually wears her hair in a bun or ponytail but today the long grey strands are braided down one side. Her eyes are a little tired around the edges but full of life and strength, just like Nan. She opens her arms and I practically dive into them. She strokes my hair and kisses the top of my head.

"How was the first solo meeting, kiddo?" She says, pushing me back gently so she can see my face. I'd forgotten about the meeting.

Today sucked.

I want to cry. That's not really saying much, I usually want to cry. I'm a cryer.

"Good. Georgina stole my hat and Marybeth hated my cookies." I smile through watery eyes and Nan laughs. Her laugh is so full of everything that makes Nan, Nan. Pure light and energy.

"That sounds about right," she says.

I swing my legs up onto the couch and she wraps her arms around me. I have never cared that I am sixteen and shouldn't be cuddling with my grandmother. I will cuddle her any chance I get.

"So," she continues to stroke my hair, "what's wrong?"

She's good.

My eyes do fill with tears this time.

"I almost had three panic attacks today. It's just so hard. I can't do this, Nan. I'm avoiding everyone. School starts tomorrow and I'm having nightmares about it. I don't want to be anywhere near Deacon. Everything is just falling apart."

I'm breathing heavily. Trembling

everywhere. My skin feels hot but freezing at the same time. The shadows snake their way into my mind and I'm tired. I'm too tired to fight so I let the panic take me. Fragments of thoughts and flashes of visions crash around in my brain while waves of energy cause my body to rock back and forth. I let the panic suffocate me. It doesn't make any sense. The visions, fears, panic. It never makes any sense.

I'm only vaguely aware when Nan places her strong hands on either side of my face and touches her nose to mine, something she's done since I was a child. It takes me awhile but I find my way to her. My eyes dart back and forth until I see her. My gaze locks onto hers and my thoughts instantly slow. I take a deep breath and try to rein them in.

The snowball effect of the panic is the hardest to overcome but when I look into Nan's eyes her power gives me strength. She's the one who took me off the zombie meds, she's the one who believes I can over come the attacks on my own. I'm not so sure it's true but it doesn't matter now, anyway.

The attacks are getting worse. Mom wants me back on meds. I just don't have the heart to tell Nan.

The attack takes so much out of me I don't have the strength to hold myself up. I sink down and rest my head on her lap.

"Why does this happen to me?" I ask quietly even though I know she doesn't know.

There is no trauma in my past, no abuse. My parents would have to pay attention to me in order to abuse me. I've been to so many doctors and none of them know why. First it was depression, then panic disorder and now it's obsessive-compulsive disorder and mild agoraphobia. I don't even know what any of that means. Apparently the doctors don't either. At least they've never explained it to me in a way that makes sense to me.

"Because this is the way you are. You're wired this way and there's no reason why you can't learn to control them." She strokes my hair.

"I just want them to go away. I hate them so much."

She shushes me.

"Just rest for awhile, darling. You've had a long day."

My eyes flutter. It's hard to keep them open. My body feels three times heavier.

"How are *you* feeling, Nan?" I turn to her. She won't return my gaze.

"Oh, I'm fine. You have a nap, then I'll make you a nice dinner. I'll call your mother and tell her you'll stay with me tonight."

She reaches to the end of the couch and pulls a wool blanket up to my chin. I'm just too tired to question her. I know something is wrong.

Nan's as bad a liar as I am.

CHAPTER FOUR

Lachlan

I slide silently out of Gram's house sometime around midnight and push my motorbike out of the garage. I push it almost half a block before I dare to start it.

Rawlins' words bounce around in my head about what Gram did for me. Taking full legal responsibility like that. Guilt bubbles at a full rolling boil under my skin. This is no way to pay her back. I glance down at my phone again. A new text that simply says **408 10th Ave.**

That's the pick up. I growl low in my throat, wishing I could tell them to shove it. Especially now that I know what Gram did.

But I owe just as much to these guys.

This is really fucked up.

Ask for help once and this is what I get. A gig as a drug runner for the biggest dealer in town. Yeah, they say it's the last time. They've been saying that for weeks, but once I turn 18, I can't run anymore.

I shove the phone in my pocket and swing a leg over my bike. Revving the engine, the bike lurches forward.

The back tire skids along the pavement because, like everything else in my life, I push the gas a little too hard.

~

I pick up at 10th Ave all the time, so I know exactly where to go. Routine.

I slow the bike as I reach the old wooden house and pull into the cracking driveway. There's a six-foot tall fence around the yard to keep the neighbors in the dark about what goes down in this place.

I ring the bell on the outside of the fence. On the second floor of the house someone pulls the curtain, flooding the front yard with yellow light. I'm plunged back into darkness as the person comes down to let me in.

So far, everything's just as it always is. Next he'll let me in, I'll go through a check, get the package and get the address of the drop off. Basic runner duties.

Don't tell the runner anything. The less I know the harder it is for the cops to trace it back.

The fence gate swings open and I'm face to face with Garrett. He sticks his hand out and I take it. He pulls me into his chest then lets go, which is like a guy equivalent of a hug, I guess. I don't do physical contact.

"I was hoping it'd be you, Lannie." Garrett's eyes are shadowed and one of them is black. His cheeks are sunken, not from the drugs though, it's natural for him. His smile is forced and I'm sure he only likes me because I keep my mouth shut and always turn down the cut of dope I'm entitled to as the runner. I quit that shit for Gram. It's a stipulation of me being released into her care. Rehab at sixteen. Support meetings. Fun.

I step into the yard and the gate closes behind me. Garrett drapes his arm around my shoulder, or tries to, as we walk up the front steps. I'm about a foot taller than he is. I shake him off easily, without seeming like an asshole. But I am an asshole, so he doesn't notice.

"You want a hit, kid?" Garrett points to a small square mirror with a line of cocaine and a blade on it laying on a small table in the entrance.

"Nah, man. I'm good," I say and lean against the doorway into the disaster of living room.

He smiles. He knew I would turn it down.

"Just wait there. I'll be back with the package."

He's gone only a few moments when a pair of boney arms slide around my waist. I recognize the arms. They've been around me more than once. I grab her wrists and gently remove them.

"Violet, not now," I say like a mother talking to her child. When did I become this guy? I never turn down sex. Again, maybe not entirely true, but I never used to turn down sex from Violet. It's always sex with Violet.

I turn to face her, and I'm reminded of why I turn her down now.

Memories of the once beautiful and voluptuous Violet flood my body. I remember when the drugs made her wild and spontaneous. When we would get high and the sex was crazy amazing. Partying with Violet was one way I could escape the pain. She was great at making me forget. Being older than me, she was my first and definitely my best.

She presses her body into mine and my hands slide down her shoulders as I gently push her away. I wished she was the old Violet. I could use a dose of the old Violet right now.

The new Violet makes my chest constrict and digs at my conscience.

Drugs dominate the new Violet, making her frail and desperate. She's lost all her curves and all the softness that made her amazing to touch. Her eyes are faded, lifeless.

She seems already dead at nineteen, only a shell of who she used to be. Now she clings to anyone who can give her her next fix and she comes back here to Garrett, to me, when she needs money or when she gets kicked out of her house.

What terrifies me most about the New Violet is that I was right there with her. Controlled by the quest to numb out. To stop feeling. I could be this right now.

I think of Gram.

Violet doesn't respond to me when I turn her in the direction of the living room. She just wanders away. I no longer have what she wants. An escape. Violet slinks into an oversized chair and it almost swallows her, her boney arms hang limply at her sides. I realize she's not on coke, the way her jaw hangs open and her eyes won't focus are sure signs of heroin. Shit, I don't want to be part of this anymore.

Garrett comes bounding down the stairs and I almost punch him in the face, making his other eye black. I stop my twitching hand by curling my fingers into my palm.

Whatever happened to just smoking a joint in your parent's basement?

"What's your problem, man?" Garrett sees through my anger, which isn't hard to do. I'm not exactly subtle about it. My criminal record is proof of that.

"Nothing, dude. Just check me so I can get out of here." I spread my arms and legs. Garrett runs his hands along the length of my body making sure I don't have weapons or wires. He sticks his hands in my pockets, pulling my phone out to make sure it's not recording anything. He reaches under my t-shirt and pats his hand up to my chest and around to my back to make sure I'm not 'wearing' then traces up my neck and around my ears. I just stare straight ahead. I've been searched so many times by cops and guards and social workers, I'm good at blocking it out.

Technically, Garret is supposed to do this right when I walk in the door, but he knows I'm cool.

He presses the brown package into my chest and opens the front door.

"I hear your probation is up." He grabs my shoulder, "We'll be sorry to see you go, man. I've never seen anyone able to run while on probation and not get caught."

He laughs. I nod to him and leave without saying goodbye. I have no response. I'm the best and I hate myself for it.

The text comes before I even reach my bike.

754 Vista Court. Over the fence. DO NOT

go to the door.

I pull the phone closer to my face. My eyebrows burrow together as I read the address again. Vista court is the rich end. I've never done a run there before. The rich use a middleman so us lowly runners don't know who they are. But I guess if I'm just throwing it over the fence.

I glare the entire way to Vista Court, get lost twice and almost turn around and leave. Every street is named Vista something and every house looks the damn same. What is it with these people?

Finally, I find the house and throw the package over the fence. It's weird, throwing it in the yard, but I don't question it.

One, it's my job to *not* know. Two, I really don't care.

~

The air's hot and stuffy. The house doesn't have air conditioning and all I hear is the whoosh, whoosh, whoosh of the ceiling fan but it does nothing to stop the sweat from pouring off my face. I'm crouched against the wall in the far corner of our tiny living room clutching my arm. The sweat from my fingers stings the open wound. My small body is tucked behind the couch. I'm crying. Shaking. There is vomit on my t-shirt. I don't know if it's mine. Sometimes it hurts so bad I throw up.

I hear his voice and my heart slams against my ribs.

Whoosh, whoosh, whoosh. The ceiling fan spins, swirling the dusty air.

"Where is he?" he's mad. He's been drinking that brown stuff. His voice only sounds like that after he drinks the brown stuff.

I push further into the crack. Maybe he won't reach me. He doesn't try as hard when he's wobbly.

I lift my hand to look at the burn on my skin.

Smoke fills my nostrils. It hurts. The smell makes my stomach flop. The scent of burning skin.

Stronger. The pain, the smell. I want it to stop.

I press my palm on my nose but it won't go away. The smoke still lingers.

I just want it to go away.

I rock back and forth. I cry harder. The smoke gets thicker.

~

My eyes spring open as the smell of burning eggs and cheese overpower my senses. I'm leaning on my hand on Gram's vinyl countertop and must have fallen asleep.

I run to the stove through the smoke and grab the pan off the burner. It burns my hand and I drop the pan with a clatter and shake my hand.

Gram is standing in the doorway in her nightgown and robe, smiling. She hands me a dish towel and I use that to lift the pan.

"Sorry, Gram, only slightly burnt this time." I shrug and begin to dish out the eggs onto a plate. I shake the lingering dream from my mind. It's been awhile since I dreamt of him.

We eat in silence but Gram keeps glancing up at me and her eyes darken only for a moment before she smiles, and I smile back. Silence is very unlike Gram, she's a woman who speaks her mind and it makes me nervous how quiet she is.

I move around the kitchen cleaning up breakfast but she's always watching. It's unnerving so I leave the dishes and get ready for school.

I have a quick shower and a smell of all the T-shirts on my floor to see which one's the cleanest, settling on plain white. I don't let Gram into my room, or wash my clothes. She does enough for me already. I have no idea how to pay her back so I make sure I don't let her do anymore than she has to.

Gram holds a backpack out as I make my way to the front door. Grabbing it, I shake my head and toss it into the corner of the front closet. I don't do school work so no need for a backpack.

I push my feet into my sneakers without undoing the laces and Gram clears her throat. I walk over and give her a quick one-armed hug and kiss her forehead, like I do every morning.

"Lachlan, son, I want you to come home right after school. I need to talk to you about all this sneaking out you've been doing."

My jaw muscles all fail at the same time and I look down at my frail grandmother, her boney hands resting on her hips.

"Don't look at me like that," she says. "I'm an 80-year-old woman who had a husband and 4 children. Don't think you can pull the wool over my eyes that easy, young man. Be home, or we're going to have problems."

"Yes, Gram." I say with total sincerity. I never want to have problems with Gram. I'm terrified of what that could mean.

CHAPTER FIVE

Talia

The first day of school is my worst nightmare. In the literal sense, I'm still having nightmares about it.

I text Janna when I wake up. She always has her phone, I swear she sleeps with it pressed to her ear, but I still haven't heard from her.

I hate first days, and I've already had a panic attack that left me curled up on my bed, exhausted. I'm used to this. I also have night terrors all the time, the doctor says it's part of the anxiety. I say it is because my brain is revolting against me. I'm used to it, but that doesn't mean it doesn't suck big time.

I brush my teeth like a zombie and can't stop the dark shadows of my thoughts from closing in. They slither and slide through my brain, tainting everything with doom.

I can't shake the feeling that the actual

first day of school isn't going to be far from the nightmare version, so I take my time getting ready. I eat breakfast at a glacial pace as my mother sits across the table from me, painting her long fake fingernails. She looks up once. Once. But hasn't said a word. Part of me wishes she'd talk to me, part of me is glad that she just stays out of it. When she does talk to me it's about going back on pills. I don't tell her about the attacks anymore. I used to call out to her but now we barely speak.

"So when is dad getting home?" I ask, trying to make conversation. She smiles at me but it's fake and it doesn't reach her eyes. My mother is very pretty. Tall and skinny like Nan but she has Pop's brown eyes and light hair.

"On Saturday maybe."

"Maybe?" How does she not know when her husband is getting home? Sometimes I feel like we're just roommates, the three of us, instead of a family. It didn't used to be this way. I remember when my dad was a defense lawyer and mom and I would go watch him in court. Now he settles accounts and writes contracts for some corporate insurance company and we never see him anymore.

"It depends on how the negotiations go,

Tali. He might have to stay, or he might be able to come home."

"I bet he just has another family," I mumble and dump my bowl into the sink.

"What was that?" Mom glances up from her nails and narrows her eyes.

"Nothing."

I don't think I'd be surprised if he does have another family.

I put on a grey hat I'd knit a long time ago with Nan and adjusted it, tucking in my bangs. I lift my bag over my shoulder and push my headphones onto my head. I don't say goodbye to my mom. I never do.

~

The school looks the same as it did last year, and the year before. Eleventh grade won't be any different than the 10th, I'm sure. We're not the youngest, not the oldest, just there. No need to panic. I am alone, but that's okay. I'm always alone. Except for Janna, who usually helps me through first days. I wonder why she hasn't text me back yet.

Girls giggle behind me and despite myself I turn to see what it's about. I don't even notice the girls because my eyes are glued to a black and silver motorbike and it's tall, tattoo-covered rider. I try to turn away but he sees me and I freeze. No one ever sees me.

Lachlan hangs his helmet on the handlebars of his bike and reaches into his back pocket. He pulls out my hat and sets it on his head. His dark curls flatten around his face and hang over his thick eyebrows. The intensity of his gaze makes me shiver, but not in a good way. He's wearing jeans, a white t-shirt that's frayed around one arm and a leather wristband on the other tattoo-covered arm. I had heard once that he has to wear the band because, whatever is tattooed underneath, the school won't let him leave it uncovered. But I hear a lot of things about Lachlan. Most of them straight up ridiculous. He can't be a drug King Pin, he's in high school. I also highly doubt he's as big of a player as people say, with college girls none the less. Why would any college girl want a senior in high school?

The giggling girls snap me out of my thoughts and I realize I'm staring.

Lachlan walks up the concrete pathway and half his mouth turns into a grin. I look behind me. Yup. He's grinning at me.

I should just walk away but instead, like the awesomely cool person I am not, I stand and stare.

"Talia, right?" he asks pointing. I nod. I'm blushing. He puts his hand on my shoulder, "Thanks for the hat. Make sure Gram pays you for it, okay?"

He winks and disappears into the school. My face is on fire, not because Lachlan had talked to me, but because the giggle trio are staring with mouths open.

"You gave him that hat?" The tallest blonde one asked. My face burns hotter. People don't notice me. People aren't supposed to notice me.

"Actually, I made it. His Grandma stole it from me." Why did I just say that? This is why I stay invisible.

The three girls exchange a sideways glance and then frown in unison. I don't wait for them to respond. My breathing speeds up.

Not again.

I switch direction quickly and try not to sprint around the side of the huge brick school. Chills travel the length of my body and my hands are shaking. I round the corner to find a spot to just stop and breathe. I walk straight in on a make-out session.

I stop, alright. Everything stops. Time stops. The shaking stops.

I gawk at the two startled faces that stare back at me. It seems like hours before I recognize them.

"Deacon?" I ask. A stupid question because I am well aware it's Deacon.

Why do people ask stupid questions?

"Talia!" Janna shoves Deacon away from her. Her eyes are wide and there are tears sliding down her cheeks.

"Talia, babe..." Deacon starts but I raise my hand. Janna slides down the wall until she's sitting in the dirt. Her shoulders are shaking. Her hand is over her mouth. She won't look at me. I turn back to Deacon.

"Nope."

It's all I can think of to say. I turn on my heel and walk away.

I should be panicking. This is the perfect moment to panic, but the tricky thing about panic attacks is they never happen when they are supposed to. I am in too much shock to feel anything really.

I storm towards the bike rack, my shoulder slamming into someone I don't see. I have tunnel vision. I just need to get out of here.

I hear footsteps behind me, "Talia!" Deacon grabs my arm.

I turn.

He stands in front of me, his sandy hair hanging around his face, but his expression doesn't look any different than normal.

"She's my best friend, Deacon. She's my only friend." My voice is less than a whisper.

"That was nothing," He shrugs.

Did he seriously just shrug? I yank my arm

from his grip.

"That didn't look like nothing." I cross my arms. My lip trembles and I chew on it.

"If you'd let me explain," Deacon's voice is hard, like I'm the one at fault for not letting him talk.

"Go away, Deacon." I need to get out of here. I need to see Nan. I start walking away again.

Deacon grabs my arm, harder this time, and spins me around to face him. It hurts and I try to yank my arm free.

From out of nowhere, Lachlan steps in between us and pushes Deacon out at arms length, his long fingertips on Deacon's chest. His other hand is on my stomach. I feel nauseous. He's shielding me with his body.

"If I heard correctly, I think the lady told you to go away." Lachlan's voice is low and serious, but unnervingly calm. Even more unnerving is that his tone soothes me. I feel calmer, stronger. His southern accent is faint but there's a slight twang in his voice that I didn't notice yesterday. I never knew he was from the South, but that is ridiculous. I don't know anything about him.

Why am I thinking about this?

My stomach won't stop flopping around, but the pressure of Lachlan's hand helps a little.

Deacon watches me from around Lachlan. I look at my shoes. When I lift my head up again my now ex-boyfriend is gone. Lachlan grins and raises one eyebrow.

"Trouble in paradise?" The twang is gone.

I scoff and unlock my bike. "You could say that."

"You want to get out of here?" he asks and points to his bike. I must have a horrified look on my face because he laughs. Really loudly.

"This isn't where I take you out of town and murder you, Hat Girl. Our grandparents know each other, someone would find out. I prefer to murder people my Gram doesn't have a crush on."

I feel my face burn again. That's not what I thought.

"Um, no. I mean, no thanks." I swing a leg over the seat and push my bike forward. Away from Lachlan. I can hear him laughing behind me. The burn in my face changes from embarrassment to anger.

Guys *are* jerks.

~

I pedal at hard as I can until I reach Nan's house.

I'm such an idiot.

Tears pour from my eyes. I can barely see to get to the door.

Janna. How could she?

Sobs come so forcefully that my breath catches in my throat, and I have to choke out each individual lungful of air. I collapse onto the front step and pull my knees to my chest.

My body rocks back and forth.

I don't know how much time passes.

A warm hand touches my hair and Nan makes clucking noises with her tongue as she sits down beside me. I didn't even hear the door open.

"Darling? Darling, what's wrong?" She tries to pull my head up to look at her, but I just bury my face deeper into my arms. I am so embarrassed. I should have noticed at the pool. How could this happen to me?

Nan runs her fingers through my hair while I cry and clench and unclench my fists.

Finally, I take a couple deep breaths. My head is throbbing and I can feel my eyes swelling.

"Okay, now tell me what's wrong? Shouldn't you be at school?" Nan places her hand under my chin and my eyes fill with tears again.

"Deacon... and he... kissing her... how could he... my best friend..." I try to get it out in one sentence but my voice keeps breaking.

Nan nods her head and wipes at my tears with her thumb.

"Did you love him, darling?" She asks calmly. I sit back.

"What?" I wipe my eyes with the heels of my hands.

"Did you love him?"

"Um, I don't know. No. We'd only been dating for the summer..."

Nan tilts her head to one side.

"Did you love her?"

"Janna?" I'm still confused. "Yeah. I loved Janna."

"Well then cry for her. Not him."

I open my mouth and then close it again before any excuses escape.

"Those we love are the only ones worth crying over," Nan continues. She reaches out her hand and I take it. She wraps her other arm around my shoulders and I lean against her.

"Now that's not to say it doesn't sting. That's not to say you can't hate the cheating bastard for a while. But save your tears for those you love. For all the Jannas that you lose."

I rest my head on her shoulder and she kisses the top of my head. Sometimes I wish she'd agree with me. Or give me permission to hate the world and everyone in it.

"I thought the saying is those who love you will never make you cry?"

Nan laughs making her cough a raspy cough.

"Oh good heavens girl, what fantasy land are you living in?" she says after she recovers. Her eyes sag. She wheezes faintly with each exhale.

My eyebrows pull together.

"In the one where guys are decent."

And Nans don't lie.

She smiles with her mouth but her eyes are dull.

"They're not all bad, darling. Someday you'll see that."

CHAPTER SIX
Lachlan

Straight home after school. Just like Gram said. I jog up the front porch humming a tune she used to sing to me as a kid.

Shutting the door behind me, I throw my keys in the bowl by the front door. I kick my shoes off and hang my helmet on the peg that Gram dedicated for it. Heaven help me should I hang anything on *her* peg.

"Gram! I'm home. 3:30 on the dot." I listen and hear nothing. I also smell nothing, which is really weird. Gram's place always smells of food.

"Gram?" I step into the living room. The radio is playing softly in the background, but otherwise silence. My heart beats a little faster.

"Where are you?" I call louder. Nothing.

I fly down the hallways and to her bedroom. I push the door too hard and it hits the wall with a crunch, the handle piercing through the drywall. I scan Gram's room.

Nothing.

"Lachlan?" a small voice sounds behind me. I turn. No one in the hallway.

"Gram?"

"Lachlan, I'm in the bathroom. I fell down, son. Can you please help me?"

I burst into the bathroom without thinking and immediately spin around, throwing my forearm across my eyes.

"Hand me a towel, will ya?" her voice is pleasant. The woman falls naked in the bathtub and has been laying there for who knows how long and she says *hand me a towel, will ya?*

I grab the towel from the rack and reach behind me so she can take it. When she's covered I turn to help her up and out of the tub. I wrap her robe around her and hug her tightly to me. She's shivering.

"Good thing I fell so I could turn the water off."

I hold her at arms length. Her lips are bluish but she's smiling.

"Good thing...? Gram you could have broken something... you could have cracked your head open."

"Oh, don't be such a drama queen. I'm fine."

I hug her again, rubbing my hands on her arms to warm her up. I lead her to her room and sit in the living room while she changes. When she sits down next to me a few minutes later she's still shivering so I wrap a blanket around her and get her slippers. I slam my way around the kitchen to make her tea.

"Come on, Lachlan. I didn't mean to fall. Don't be angry with me."

I stop and my stomach sinks. The last thing I could ever be is mad at Gram. I lean back to see around the wall that divides the kitchen and living room.

"I don't think you should shower or bathe unless I'm here, Gram."

She makes a funny sound and waves her hand. I set the cup down and move to kneel in front of my grandmother.

I take her hands in mine and she looks down at me with wide eyes. I don't make gestures like this often so she better listen.

"Grandma Georgina, you are the only person I have on this earth. Nothing can happen to you, okay? If something happens to you, I'll have no one."

She pats my hand then takes my face into her hands, as she did when I was a kid.

"How about we just get some of those old lady railings installed so I have something sturdy to hold onto?"

I smile. "I can handle that."

She rubs my cheek and I go back to making tea.

~

"So you were planning on giving me shi–um, scolding me for something this morning?" Spending time in Juvie really makes it hard to clean up the language. She doesn't seem to pick up on it, so I continue. "Let's just get it over with then."

Gram sets her tea down and purses her lips together. Her thinking face makes me nervous so I react like I always do when I'm nervous–I lean back in my chair and act like I could care less about what she has to say.

"Where have you been sneaking out to? Is it for a girl?" She folds her hands in her lap.

I play with the bottom of my t-shirt, and adjust the leather band buckled around my wrist. I don't want to say it's a girl, because I don't sneak around for girls, but it would break her heart if I told her I'm indebted to a drug dealer and run narcotics all over the city for them.

I stretch and put my hands on top my head, the wool hat tickling my fingers.

I think of Hat Girl.

"Yeah, Gram. A girl." I can't meet her eyes or she'd know I'm lying.

"Well I'd like you to break it off with this girl. Any girl who sneaks around in the night is not good for you."

I nod and force back a smirk. Next thing she'll say is to go steady and give my class ring to the head cheerleader.

"And, you are grounded."

This makes me laugh. I look up at her and she's frowning.

"Gram, I've been on Probation for the last two years... It's pointless to ground me."

"Right, then. I'm helping Talia plan the Christmas Charity Drive for my knitting club, you'll help us too. That way I can keep a closer eye on you."

I stop laughing, "No way, Gram. I love you, but not a chance."

She narrows her eyes and sits up as straight as her crooked spine will let her. Her look of cold disappointment travels the length of me.

"I wasn't asking." She tosses the blanket from her shoulders and carries her teacup to the kitchen.

I nod even though she can't see me.

"Yes, Gram."

CHAPTER SEVEN

Talia

Now that I don't have a boyfriend, or a best friend, it's way easier to go about my days completely unnoticed. After the freak out on day one, I've managed to stay invisible all week. I also haven't had as many panic attacks. It's like the less I allow people into my life the better I feel. And, I feel okay today. It's just me and Nan.

I sit at her kitchen island and knit. The only sound in the room is my knitting needles clacking together as I work on my fifth hat this week. I'm hoping to finish one more hat by the meeting tomorrow as well as come up with a really good reason why I can't plan the charity drive.

"What do you have there, darling?" Nan asks, leaning over the island. This is the first time she's gotten off the couch. She's worn out, I can see it in every movement she makes. She still won't admit that something's wrong.

I'm just about to press her for details again but she's wiggling her fingers. I place my half done hat in her hands and get nervous as she inspects it. I just wish she'd tell me what's wrong.

"This is lovely. What is it?" She looks over her glasses. She only wears them when she knits.

I force a laugh.

"It's a hat, like the other one I showed you. This one has a skull on it, though."

"Why in heaven's name would you put a skull on a hat?"

"People like it. I have one with a flower too, for those who aren't into skulls."

"I don't understand how anyone can be 'into' skulls."

I stand up and pull the edge of my tiny skull covered underwear out of my jeans and Nan presses her lips together and frowns. I laugh and tucked them back in.

"I don't know, Nan. I just like them, but I only have socks and underwear. I leave the death skulls to the more hardcore."

Nan shakes her head and continues to scan the hat.

"This is really wonderful, darling. I'm so proud of what you've learned."

"I'd like to sell them at the drive. Maybe

then someone under the age of 50 will actually show up." I smirk and Nan sticks her tongue out at me.

"I think you should. After all, you're planning it."

I blush, I hope I won't be planning it. I hope that she just gets better and then rocks the show like she always does.

"Don't you have to have the work juried?"

"I'm sure you'll be fine. It's just a hat, and you are a good enough knitter. But maybe submit the one with the flower for jurying. After you're accepted you can put whatever your twisted heart desires on the hats."

She hands the hat back and heads back to the couch, which is her favorite place to knit. I feel the most calm when I am knitting with Nan. It's like all the jumbled thoughts move to the back of my brain and I can think clearly.

But I'm still dreading the meeting tomorrow.

~

Dad's home when I wake up on Sunday morning. He's reading the paper, playing with the side of his glasses. He glances up when I pad into the room. He does that thing with his mouth that looks like it could be a smile, but he's a lawyer so it's neutral looking and I can't really tell.

I get my cereal and milk and sit down across from him. I've never realized how young he looks. He has a full head of thick dark hair, like mine, and there are only a few faint lines around his eyes.

"So how was your trip?" I ask, still studying his face but this time I'm searching for expression. Particularly a guilty one.

He looks up with his permanent impartial expression, "Fine. How was your first week of school? I feel bad for missing your first day."

I choke on my last bite of cereal. I can't remember the last time he asked me a question, never mind apologized to me for missing something.

Sure, if I ramble on about something he'll listen...kind of, but he doesn't start the conversations.

"Deacon cheated on me with Janna, so I dumped him and don't have a best friend anymore. And, a senior at school tried to get me to go on a motorcycle with him. He has tattoos and has been to prison. So all-in-all pretty good."

I smile at my dad's stare of incredulity. It feels good to make a lawyer lose his composure. Although, he'll probably never ask me another question again.

"I'm, I'm sorry to hear that. Deacon was a

nice kid," he recovers quickly. He's a good lawyer.

"Not really if he cheats on his girlfriend, Dad."

He frowns like I'm crazy.

"I guess not."

I dump my left over milk in the sink. I hug him quickly and kiss his temple.

"Nice to have you home, Dad."

He forces a confused half smile before going back to his paper.

~

I ride my bike to the Wool Shop and lock it up in my regular spot. I didn't bring cookies this week, because...well, because I didn't want to. I'm not Nan, I don't have time to bake cookies every week. I asked her to bake them for me when I called her this morning to double check that she was missing another meeting but she said she was tired. She says that a lot now and I am positive that something's going on that I don't know about. It's driving me crazy. She's not being herself and I'm worried about her. Nan has always been the only thing I *didn't* worry about.

I push open the door into the familiar warmth of the shop. Immediately I sense something is different. I scan the store, music still blaring though my headphones. I spot the hat first, then the soft curls, then the defined jaw and sharp nose. Lachlan is definitely not movie star gorgeous, but there's something about him that demands attention. I would be lying if I said I didn't like looking at him.

He sees me and grins. His mouth moves, then he gets up and walks toward me. He lifts one ear of my headphones and puts his face close enough to mine that I can feel his breath on my skin. The scent of toothpaste fills my nose and the minty air stings my eyes.

"Nice to see you again, Talia," he whispers as I stab at the buttons of my music player, trying to make it stop.

"Good taste, Hat Girl," he continues. "This band is pretty badass."

He replaces the earpiece on my ear and sits back down. All the other ladies are watching me, except Marybeth. Marybeth is glaring.

I push my headphones down and make my way to the couches in the middle of the room. Nan's chair is the only one open. Lachlan's in mine. I glance around the room and most of the ladies have gone back to their knitting or their conversations about knitting, but Marybeth is still glaring.

"Sorry I didn't bring the cookies,

Marybeth. I just don't..."

Lachlan puts his hand out to stop me and points his thumb at Marybeth.

"She's pissed that I'm here," Lachlan says. Georgina reaches out and smacks him with her knitting needle. Marybeth's glare deepens, and I have to move my eyes away from her so I don't laugh. I connect with Lachlan's gaze and he wiggles his eyebrows. My lips stretch into a smile. A real smile. It feels weird, but nice. I would ask if I sound crazy, but according to the doctors, I am.

"Anyways," he starts, not taking his eyes off me. "I'm only here to say I've been bullied into helping with this artsy thing..."

Georgina hits him with the needle again.

"Okay, Gram, Jeez. I've been asked nicely to help you and I came by to say I would be honored to sell your doilies for you."

Lachlan leans toward me, his elbows on his knees. He's thin but muscular, like a hockey player, except I doubt he ever played hockey. He holds his hand out to me and I hesitate before I give him mine. He curls my fingers in his and presses his lips to the back of my hand.

I will my face to stay its natural colour, but goosebumps spring up along my arms at the light touch of his lips.

"I'm at your beck and call, m'lady." His

slight accent comes out in full force. He bows as he stands up and lets my hand go slowly, our fingertips sliding apart. "How was that, Gram?"

She beams at him. "Be back in two hours so we can make our plans."

~

Two hours fly by but I can't push Lachlan from my mind. The only thing I have the guts to ask is where he picked up that accent. Apparently he's from Louisiana somewhere. The conversation never went farther than that. I'm confused as to why I want it to go further. I just can't stop thinking about him.

I drop six stitches and have to start over twice as I show Anna how I do the cabling for the hat I'm working on. I stretch out my fingers then ball my hand into a fist before I continue knitting. The skin on the back of my hand still tingles. I have no idea what is wrong with me. I don't even like him. He terrifies me more than anything. And now I have to plan a craft show with him? A craft show I don't even want to plan.

The door jingles and so does my stomach. Lachlan sits down in my chair and leans back stretching his arms out and resting them on his head.

"Times up. Let's plan a party, Gram."

I study Lachlan and the way he slouches in

his chair and grins like he doesn't care about anything, like it's no big deal he's here. There's something off about Lachlan and it tugs at that girly part of me that needs to know, that needs to find out which of the rumors are true and how much of his reputation is based on gossip.

The other ladies begin to pack up their things and Marybeth glares at Lachlan the entire time she wraps up her yarn.

I put plastic caps on the tips of my needles, so the yarn doesn't slip off, and pack up my own things. I pull a notebook from my bag, and Georgina hands me a pen.

"Okay, so the craft show is the first weekend in December," I start. My breath catches. That's not as far as it seems. I crack my wrist a couple times and tap my pen on the paper.

Lachlan groans. I tilt my head to the side. *Really?*

Georgina obviously hadn't told him that part. But it should be obvious. I glare at him.

"It's a Christmas charity event. When did you think it would be?"

He stares. His head angles to match mine, and something changes in his eyes. I'm not sure he's used to being talked to this way. I don't have time for this. All he has to do is show up and lift some boxes. My eyes flicker to his arms, crossed in front of his chest. I immediately drop my gaze to my notepad.

The shadows are pressing at the edges of my brain. I tap my pen a few times.

"Touché, let's get on with it," he grumbles.

"Which gives us twelve weekends to get everything done." That's really not much time at all. I push air out of my lungs slowly, trying to control my breathing. I can't panic right now. Not in front of him.

Lachlan groans again and then bites his lip. His dark eyes flicker as if to say, 'Ooops'.

"We have to meet with the director of the show, get our work juried, decide how many booths we want, decide the theme, set a sales goal, volunteer at the Shelter..."

Lachlan cuts me off.

"Whoa, back it up, Hat Girl. Volunteer at the Shelter?"

"Yeah, the contributors are asked to volunteer both time and money. This is the biggest craft event of the year. The Shelter staff are a lot of fun." I try to sound light but he's irritating me and it's causing nervous energy to build inside my mind.

"I think I was led in here on false pretenses, Gram. I didn't know there would be volunteering."

"Well, you just think about that next time you want to be dishonest with me and try to play me for a fool. I can play that game, too." Georgina crosses her frail arms across her chest and Lachlan's face turns three shades of red. Fury flashes behind his dark eyes and his jaw muscle twitches but he just slouches further into his chair. He doesn't say another word the entire meeting. As soon as we're done, Lachlan's out the door without a glance in our direction.

"I'm sorry about Lachlan, Talia. He's been so misguided his whole life that it's just hard to rein him in, you know?"

I nod, but I don't know. I have no clue.

CHAPTER EIGHT

Lachlan

I clutch the steering wheel until my knuckles turn white. I want to punch something but I just hold on. As long as my hands stay on the wheel I'll be fine.

"Did I embarrass you in front of Talia?" Gram says about half way home.

"I don't care about her," I snap.

I know that hurts her feelings and I instantly regret saying it. I just can't control myself when I'm mad.

"Did you ever think that maybe she doesn't much care for you either because you act like a big pig-headed buffoon around her? All that girl cares about is making her grandma proud by doing her job as leader of our group. Now that may not seem like a big deal to you, Lachlan, but to her it is. So I would suggest you smarten up and start acting like a man, not a boy."

I'm not sure how to react. I'm not

surprised that Talia doesn't like me, I'm surprised that I care.

I turn to Gram and smirk.

"Did you just call me a pig-headed buffoon?"

"I most certainly did." She smiles.

The only person I can never stay angry with is Gram. If this girl is important to Gram, then I will do what I can to help.

If nothing else Talia has an ass worth staring at for twelve weekends.

"Sorry, Gram."

"You've been saying that a lot lately."

We drive in silence the rest of the way home.

~

The text comes at 8pm.

408 10th Ave

I slide my phone back into my pocket and stick my head into the living room.

"Hey Gram, I'm going to run to the store and grab some ice cream. You want anything?"

"No thanks." She doesn't look at me and I'm glad.

I slip my shoes on and head to the garage. The guilt of lying to Gram again fills my thoughts. I'm not paying attention as I push my motorbike out onto the street and almost run over Talia.

"What are you doing here?" I hiss at her and by the hurt expression on her face I'm guessing it came out wrong.

She slams the box she's holding into my chest. I brace my bike with my legs, trying not to drop either.

"Bringing this stuff by for Georgina. It's Nan's notes for the sale. She wants us to go over it." Her voice is tight. Her arms are straight by her side. She is so rigid. So closed off.

Gram's right, she really doesn't like me. Or maybe she's just uptight, as straight as those knitting needles she loves so much, and talks to everyone like that. I don't know, I barely know her. But something about her intrigues me. Something about the way she switches on and off. There's more to her. I've never been curious like this about someone, until this afternoon at the meeting. How her skin felt when I took her hand. How everything around her was neat and in order and her knitting needles were lined up from biggest to smallest. How, from out of nowhere, she flared to life and shut me down without even blinking.

I press the kickstand down with my heel and prop my bike on it. Steadying the box she forced into my arms, I walk back to the garage. I stop when I see the spare helmet hanging on the wall.

No way, I think. This chick would never.

But that just makes me want to try.

"Did you walk here?" I whisper.

"Yeah, I don't live too far away. Why are you whispering? Where are you going?"

I grab the second helmet off the peg. I have no idea what I'm thinking but I hold it out to her. She stares at me with those huge blue eyes and I have an overwhelming need to uproot her sheltered existence. It's an overpowering feeling and I know I should just walk away. I should leave her standing on our driveway and preserve her innocence but something about her, something about the way she looks at me, makes me want to drag her down into my world. Bring her to my level so I don't feel so alone anymore. I get the feeling that she's like me. Alone.

"Put it on," I say.

"But..."

"Please." I place the helmet on her head, clipping the strap under her trembling chin.

I flip up the bike stand and swing my leg over, kicking the bike to life. The motor rumbles, masking the thunderous sound of my heart against my ribs.

What the fuck am I doing?

"Get on." I have to yell. Talia doesn't move. I hold my hand out to her and she stares at it.

"Come on, trust me, Hat Girl."

She slowly takes my hand and I pull her to the bike. To me. She lifts her leg and adjusts herself behind me. I wrap her arm around my waist and glance over my shoulder at her. Her eyes are wide, shocked, and I get a sick sense of pleasure from it. This girl has probably never let go. She has probably never done anything wrong in her life. I grab her other hand and bring it around me too.

"Hold on," I say over the loud hum of the engine. She presses herself into my back and balls the front of my shirt into her fists. Her fingers dig into my skin.

Part of me says stop, to let her get off and go home, to tell her to forget I even exist and to never speak to me again. But another part of me feels like it's the right thing to do. I need to bring her with me. I need her with me. I hate this feeling. Even more, I hate that I don't know where this feeling is coming from.

I race through the streets, faster than I usually drive, and try to convince myself I'm not trying to scare her. Every time I take a corner too fast or hit the gas a little too hard she squeezes me tight, the entire length of her presses against me. I like it. I feel more alive than I have in months. Hell, I haven't felt this good since I was using.

I turn onto 10th Ave and stop a couple houses down from Garrett's. I want Talia with me, I just don't want her knowing what I'm doing.

I cut the engine and have to pry her arms from me. I unsnap my helmet and then hers. Helping her pull hers off first. I'm glad I did because as soon as she's free she starts hitting me. First she punches me in the chest, then slaps my arm and hits my helmet with both of her hands. I grab her hands. Her eyes are frantic and she's not focusing on me or anything else.

"Hey, hey? Talia. What's wrong?" I press her hands to my chest so she can't hit me again.

"Nan?" Her voice squeaks and she's breathing really fast, "Nan, I can't."

My eyebrows sink. What is she talking about?

She continues to ramble, the words come so fast and disjointed I can't keep up.

Great. She's gone nuts and it's my fault. I rip the helmet from my head and let it drop to the ground. It makes a loud sound and Talia jumps. She still won't focus. She's going to pass out if she keeps breathing like that.

What the hell is happening?

I'm slammed with a vision from my past. Fast breaths. Shaking. Terrified. My night terrors of him.

I grab Talia and pull her close. I lean over her and burry my face in her hair and hold her tight. Her shaking body presses against me. I have no idea why I'm doing this but it worked for me. When I was scared. Gram would hold me like this. Tight, like she could squeeze the fear out of me.

Her heavy breath heats my neck and I can't see through her thick hair. I press my cheek to hers, like Gram used to do to me. My lips are by her ear. I know what I have to do, but I'm not entirely sure why. I take a deep breath, then pause. I feel like a fucking idiot. But she's shaking so hard.

I did this. I should never have brought her. I did this to her and I need to fix it.

The tune is shaky and uneven at first but soon I am humming smoothly in her ear. It's the same tune Gram always used to calm me from my dreams. I have no idea if it will work but I did this to her. I have to try.

I move so that our foreheads are touching. I stroke her cheek and continue to hum.

Her frantic gaze finally catches mine and it's like a light switch goes on in her brain. She focuses on me and we just stare at each other. Her breath slows and the panic in her eyes dies down but they are wide. Tears slide down her face. I didn't think it was possible for me to feel like a bigger asshole. But I do.

I stroke her cheek with my thumb again then let my hand fall. She pulls back and wipes at her face with the sleeve of her sweater.

"Talia," I start. "Talia, I'm so sorry, I didn't think you'd get so upset."

She looks down into her lap and her thin pink lips turn up into a weak smile.

"No, I'm sorry. This is so embarrassing." She wipes her nose.

"What was that?" I feel like she's going to crumble to dust. I'm not too far off about how fragile she is.

"A panic attack. It's okay though, I've had them since I was a kid."

"Really. I'm so sorry," I say again, and think of Gram's words.

You've been saying that a lot lately.

"That song?" She tilts her head to the side. I'm not sure if she's talking to me or not. She's not looking at me.

"I recognize that song." This time she's talking to me.

"Gram used to sing it to me when I was a kid." I shrug, hoping she doesn't ask why. She doesn't. She pulls her eyebrows together and touches her cheek.

"Nobody's been able to help me. Nobody but Nan." She sounds confused. I think she's talking to herself again.

I open my mouth to ask what that means just as my phone buzzes in my pocket. Instead I just mutter a curse. Her head lifts but I don't meet her gaze.

I'm such a dick, and this isn't going to make me look any better.

"Listen, Talia. I have to do something really quick. I'll be two minutes then I'll take you home and you can hate me for forever, okay?"

She nods slowly. I can tell she doesn't trust me. I don't blame her.

"Two minutes." I reach out and run my hand along her cheek once more before stepping away from the bike. I don't remember the last time I've had a physical connection with someone for that long. The feel of her skin lingers on my fingertips until I ring the bell at Garrett's.

"You're late," he says when he opens the gate.

CHAPTER NINE

Talia

I should leave. I should walk away from the bike, from Lachlan, but I don't. I sit here. That tune is holding me here. Georgina's tune.

How?

I press my hand to my cheek, the last of his toothpaste lingering in my nostrils. Lachlan had calmed me. He calmed my panic. He brought me back to myself. No one but Nan has ever been able to do that. Not Mom nor Dad nor Deacon nor Janna, not anyone. It's almost enough to give me another panic attack.

I climb off his bike and sit down on the curb, hanging my head between my knees and grabbing fistfuls of my hair.

Night and day, that's what Lachlan and I are. But for some strange reason I felt like he kind of got it, even though he caused it. He didn't pull away or look at me like I was crazy. Maybe we do have something in common. The fact that no one gets us. That we're always alone.

But we're so different.

I force Lachlan from my thoughts and focus on my breathing. Expanding and contracting my chest slowly and smoothly. Counting how many seconds it takes me to breath in and out. My doctor told me it would help. It doesn't help, it just gives me something else to think about for a while. My thoughts always end up back where they started in the end.

Lachlan. The tune. Why I didn't just walk away from him in the driveway. Why I reached for his hand. How he knew what to do to help me. The pressure of his body against mine, holding me, squeezing out the panic.

I have the feeling I'm being watched and I part my hands to see Lachlan.

"You okay?" His voice shakes a little, which doesn't suit him at all. I've never heard a word come out of his mouth that wasn't dripping with confidence.

"Yeah." I try to smile. "I'm fine, really. I'm just hungry, actually. The attacks make me hungry."

Lachlan smiles and the dying sun casts

shadows across his face in all the perfect places. Definitely nice to look at.

"I know just the place."

He holds his hand out to me and I glance sideways at the bike. I do not want to get back on that thing.

"I'll go slower. I promise."

He wiggles his fingers and I let him pull me up.

He keeps his promise. I can actually see where we're going and clutch at the sides of his worn out hoodie so I can lean back a little and watch the world fly by. It's almost dark and I think about my parents. They're probably worried about me. Wait, no, they probably don't even know I'm gone.

The wind whistles in my helmet and strands of hair whip around my neck, tickling my skin. Lachlan turns onto the bridge that leads to the other side of town, the tires rumble along the pavement. The sound vibrates through me, calming my nerves in the same strange way Lachlan did.

The last hint of the sun bounces off the river and reflects back up at us. This isn't how I imagined my night and under it all I'm not sure what to make of Lachlan's actions, of my reactions or the effect he has on my anxiety. But I feel relaxed, which surprises me as much as Lachlan's ability to calm me down with just a song.

He turns and smiles, pulling me from my thoughts. He has a gorgeous smile when it's full and genuine.

~

The waitress brings the biggest piece of apple pie I've ever seen and drops two spoons on the table with a clatter. Lachlan laughs. It's full-bodied and authentic. Real. And no doubt about it, southern.

"I never said the service was great, but the pie's amazing."

"But not as good as Nan's," I say at the same time as he says, "Not as good as Gram's, of course."

We share a grin and then he leans back into the booth, laying his arm across the back of the green stuffed vinyl backrest. The laid back I-don't-care-about-anything Lachlan's back. I find myself wanting to see more of that other Lachlan. The one that speaks with an accent and holds an ocean of secrets behind those dark brown eyes. I think about asking him about that tune he sang to me but decide against it. There's more to his story but I have a feeling he's not the sharing type.

I pick up a spoon and take a small piece of pie. The warmth of the apple and coldness of the ice cream creates a soothing sensation as they mix together in my mouth. The pie is delicious, maybe even better than Nan's.

"So, why did you have to go to that house?" I ask feeling like it might be a sort of safe start.

Lachlan shifts his gaze to his spoon, twirling it in his fingers. Not nervously, just twirling it.

"No reason. A buddy lives there and I had to stop by."

I try to raise one eyebrow, but I can't raise only one eyebrow so they both go up.

"I don't buy that. But it's cool if you don't want to tell me."

I really don't know if he's lying but Nan always says if people can't look you in the eye when they answer a direct question they're lying. That and a lot of people have been lying to me lately. It won't hurt to call him on it.

"I'm not lying." Lachlan glances up at me with his eyes but his head stays down. Half of his mouth turns up into a smile and my stomach jumps.

I can't possibly. Be attracted to Lachlan McCreedy? No. He makes me uncomfortable. That's what it is.

"We should get going soon. It's getting late." I have a sudden need to get out of here, but the thought of being back on that bike, my body pressed to his, makes my heart race.

My one leg bounces under the table and it's my turn to avoid eye contact. I snap my wrists a couple times and stand up.

"You okay?" he asks.

"Mhm, fine." It's apparently my turn to lie, too.

He puts a couple bills onto the table and we leave.

"I just have to stop somewhere quick. Two minutes, I promise. Then I'll take you home."

I purse my lips together. I shouldn't care what he's up to but I do. I hold onto his waist and argue with myself about whether I want to be closer or farther away from him as he drives his motorbike to the outskirts of the city. This neighborhood is familiar to me. Why would Lachlan need to stop in Vista?

Lachlan pulls up to one of the smaller houses on the block but it's still huge. He hops off the bike and walks to the edge of the yard. He lobs something into the air over the fence. I frown at him as he walks back toward me.

"What?" He asks.

"Why did you just throw something into Deacon's backyard?"

Every feature on his face moves either straight up or straight down. The color drains.

"That's Deacon's place. That little fuckin'

punk you used to date?"

My frown deepens. "Technically you're the punk, Lachlan. Deacon has never been to prison. He also doesn't go around visiting creepy houses at night and throwing things into peoples yards."

Lachlan runs his hands through his hair.

"I shouldn't have brought you."

"Probably not."

"This isn't good."

I grab a handful of his hoodie as he paces by me and tug on it. He stops.

"Why, Lachlan? Why are you in trouble?" I know it's no use, but I am going to try anyway.

He shakes his head and continues to pace. I sigh. And I think I'm messed up.

"I can't help you if you won't tell me." I shrug and snap the chinstrap of my helmet shut.

"I don't need help." His demeanor changes, his arms fold across his chest and he leans back on one leg. We're obviously back to Mr. Cool.

"Sure you don't." I hand him his helmet from where it hangs on the handlebars.

I'm hit with a realization as I watch him put on his helmet. He's glancing at me, his eyes darting back and forth. He wants something from me. He has to or he never would have brought me here. I just wish I knew what it was.

He drives me home. It's much tenser than earlier. I feel his body rigid and stiff against my chest.

The lights are out when we get to my house, which means my parents clearly weren't concerned. I hand him back his helmet and he clips it on the bike. He watches me for a moment then his eyebrows furrow.

"Listen, Talia. I'm sorry again, about, you know." There is a heaviness to his shoulders as they hunch forward. The facade he's hiding behind cracks open just for a second and I see something I never would have thought I'd see on him. An exhaustion I recognize. The effort it takes to keep everything and everyone out and the terror of what would happen if maybe, just maybe, it's time to let someone else in.

He's so broken. He's so broken it makes me feel better. I know that makes me sound awful but I'm happy to know there's someone out there just as messed up as me. Someone who is just as tired of trying to shut it all out. Now I wonder what's the 'it' he's keeping out.

I reach out to touch his arm but stop myself halfway there and let my hand fall.

"You didn't know."

~

Lachlan's missing from school for most of the week and surprisingly I've been watching for him. I keep catching myself humming Georgina's tune. The one he used to help me calm down. For the fifth time, I look over my shoulder down the hall. I shouldn't be thinking about him right now.

I groan and continue rifling through my locker for the Math text that I lose on purpose. I see jeans and white sneakers walk up beside me. My heart thuds once in my chest and then stops beating altogether. What is wrong with me? Seriously! Deacon never made my heart jump like that and he was my *boyfriend.*

I close the locker with a clang and see Lachlan's crooked smile. He's wearing a bright red, but worn Sam Roberts T-shirt, which impresses me. He has his hands in the pockets of his faded jeans and leans against the lockers. I notice that the leather band he always wears around his wrist has some sort of symbol on it.

"Hey, Hat Girl, my eyes are up here." I hear the laughter in his voice and my face burns.

My head jerks upwards and I glare.

"What does that symbol mean on your bracelet?" I ask quickly. The last thing I need is for him to think I'm staring at his crotch.

He lifts his arm up, his tattoos stretching as his forearm flexes. The ones with the torn skin are horrifying but I can't look away.

"First of all, it's not a bracelet. It's a wristband. Got that, Hat Girl?" He pokes me in the shoulder, but I'm distracted by the three girls that are watching us with laser vision on the other side of the hall. The giggle trio from the first day of school.

"Second of all," he continues. "Come out with me tonight and maybe I'll tell ya."

What?

I have to swallow to keep my heart from beating right out of my mouth.

"Uh." My eyes snap back to him. I hug my textbook closer to me as my breathing speeds up to match my heart. "I, uh, can't."

I turn and walk away as fast as I can. Lachlan asked me out and I said NO. No one says no to Lachlan. Wait, I don't know that, but he has this aura that says he's not used to hearing no. The look he gave me proves it. I don't even know why I said no. I'm not doing anything tonight, except knitting with Nan.

Although when I talked to her this morning she wasn't too enthusiastic about my planned visit.

"You know you're always welcome here, darling." The strain was evident. "But I'll just be resting so I won't be much fun today."

I could have said yes.

No. No, I can't go on a date with him. If it was even a date. Maybe it wasn't a date. I feel stupid for thinking it was. He was probably just asking as a friend.

I duck into the first bathroom I see and go straight to the sink. I squeeze my eyes closed and force my breathing to slow. I hate this. I hate that panic controls me.

Someone clears their throat behind me. I look up into the mirror and see the color drain from my face.

"Janna, hey." I force my voice to stay even. Janna tucks a long red strand behind her ear. I can't bring myself to face her, so I just watch her reflection in the mirror.

"Hey, Tal. How are you?" Her eyes shift from the floor to me and back to the floor.

I really don't have time for this.

"Fine." I turn to leave. Is there nowhere sacred in this stupid school where I can be alone?

Jenna grabs my arm and forces me to face her.

"Tal, listen, I know you hate me. I just wanted to say I'm sorry. To your face, you know?"

I feel my thoughts start to blend together as both panic and anger swirl inside me. The jumbled mess that is my mind spins until I land on Nan and something she had said to me when I was ten.

"If you were really sorry, Janna, you wouldn't have done it." I yank my arm away.

She looks at her feet again. She sniffs hard and rubs the heel of her hand on her eye. She's trying not to cry. Janna never cries.

"This is for the best. It sucks that you hate me but you have no idea-" She stops to regain her composure again.

My body is vibrating and I want to shake my wrists. Crack my knuckles. Run a marathon. Anything to get the surge of energy out of me.

"Have no idea about what? About how my best friend went behind my back and hooked up with my boyfriend? How's *that* for the best."

She leans back against the stall and meets my eyes directly for the first time. There's something in her eyes I've never seen before. A look I can't place because it feels so foreign on her smooth and confident features. There's something going on in her head I can't figure out.

"No Tal, you have no idea who Deacon is. You never came out of your shell long enough to see it, but I guess I didn't see it either." She averts her eyes again.

"See what?" I'm not sure I want to know.

The long and painful sigh that escapes her confirms that I probably don't want to hear the answer. I cross my arms to try and stop the vibration pulsing through my body.

"That I wasn't the only one. That you were just an experiment for him. You're so closed off and he thought it would be interesting to see how far he could get with you. I swear I didn't know at first."

"At first?" I shake harder. Never mind that I was some sexual experiment. Janna knew about it? I sink into the darkest corners of my mind. This is worse than a panic attack. This isn't just a panic induced vision. This is real.

So why am I not flipping out? Why do I get a sudden wave of guilt? Why am I feeling sorry for her?

Janna steps closer and tries to take my hand.

"You don't understand, Tali. He made me keep it a secret. I hate myself for it, but you have no idea-" She stops again choking back her emotion. Janna's good at locking it away. I'm glad because I'm tired of hearing the excuses.

I step back. "You keep saying that, but I think it's pretty obvious what you did. You lied to me Janna. Deacon wanted to make a fool out of me and you let him. *You let him.*" I draw out the last words just to make sure it sticks. I can't stand it anymore. I can't hear one more word. I spin around and leave Janna standing alone in the middle of the bathroom. The guilt still gnawing at me but I should have no reason to feel guilty. I'm the one that was lied to. By Deacon, by Janna.

By Nan...

I don't have any time to dwell on my revelation that everyone I know is lying to me because as soon as I step out of the door I feel him.

Worst. Day. Ever.

"Girls spend an inordinate amount of time in the bathroom, don't they?" Lachlan is leaning against the wall. He's so laid back and I hate him. Doesn't he care about anything?

Okay, fine I'm jealous. At this moment, I'm wound so tight I can feel the edges of my body and soul start to fray. I will all of my tears to dry up because I can't let him see them. He probably thinks I am such a baby. I'm totally a baby.

"You know what inordinate means, good for you," I mumble and stalk off. He hurries to catch up and grabs my elbow. Not roughly, like Janna had, but gently. He doesn't yank me to a stop but slows me down until I have no choice but to stop and turn to face him.

I'm shocked to see the cocky smile gone and in its place pursed lips, a furrowed brow and hurt look in his eyes.

"Just because I've been to Juvie doesn't mean I'm stupid."

He moves with me when I try to turn away keeping his eyes on mine. I shouldn't have said that. If anyone is stupid it's me, not knowing that my boyfriend and best friend were hooking up right under my nose. That my boyfriend was just plain hooking up. I'm suddenly really ashamed of what I did with Deacon. I can't believe I almost had sex with him. I was just a game. And here I am judging Lachlan.

"Sorry." I force the corners of my mouth up and he returns the gesture.

"Hey, that's my line."

I smile genuinely that time and make my way to my next class. He doesn't follow me.

"I know where you live, Hat Girl," Lachlan yells down the hallway and I want to die. Everyone turns to gawk.

"And I'm taking you out tonight. See you at seven."

I finally get the nerve to glance back, but Lachlan is gone. I crack my wrists.

Arrogant jerk, I think, but a small smile bites at the corner of my mouth.

CHAPTER TEN
Lachlan

I'm not sure what possessed me to scream at her down the hallway. Maybe because I knew it would embarrass her and I feel like she could use a little more practice. Maybe because she's so damn serious about everything I wanted to make a joke. Maybe I like her. Maybe.

There is something about her I can't shake. I don't know if I'm attracted to her, not that she isn't attractive; she just isn't my usual type.

My usual type being what? Drug addled sex-fiend?

I laugh to myself as I walk to class and startle a freshman walking toward me. Her eyes go wide and she moves to the other side of the hall.

"Better hurry, Sweetie you're gunna be late." I smile at the girl. She's cute. It's also cute how her mouth turns into a startled 'O' as she tries to think of something to say. I just keep walking. I have no time for these girls. The coy games are lost on me. I like a girl who can think on her feet; has snappy comebacks.

Like Talia.

No, I can't like Talia. She's a mess and I'm a mess. What a disaster.

She does have a great ass though.

I round the corner on the way to my locker and am ambushed by three girls.

"Lachlan, right?" the blonde one says rolling her eyes up and pointing at me like she had to think about my name.

Nice try, short skirt, I think letting my eyes take in the length of her. She's way too skinny.

I nod and her two minions giggle.

Blonde stares. So I hold my hands out to the side of my body and scrunch my shoulders.

"Is that all?" I ask. All three of them exchange a glance that they seem to understand, but I don't know what it means.

"Um, no," the brunette chimes in. "We were wondering about Hat Girl?"

I feel like I'm in a different universe whenever I talk to anyone in school.

"What about her?"

I'm all for girls, and their short skirts, but sometimes it's just ridiculous.

"Could you maybe, get her to make us one?"

I laugh.

"A hat? I'm not her agent, ladies. Ask her yourself."

I step around them but Blonde grabs my arm. The one with the scars.

I yank it from her grip harder than I mean to.

Her perfectly manicured eyebrows are straight up and the glittery shadow she's wearing make her eyes appear huge and wide.

"I'm sorry." The girl still has her hand out. I try to brush it off and force a smile.

"It's cool. But seriously, Talia's cool. Just go talk to her."

I'm backing away. I hope they can't hear my heart because it's all I can hear.

The girls exchange another look. Confusion.

"I haven't seen her talk to anyone but you since the start of school."

I start to laugh but stop myself when I realize she's serious.

"No one?"

"She's kind of a loner. I don't think she likes people. Well, Janna I guess, but they're fighting I think." She looks to her friends for confirmation, but I don't give a shit about the last part.

~

Talia is waiting outside her house when I pull up in Gram's car. I figured she wouldn't be interested in another ride on the motorbike. I get out and walk around the car.

She smiles, her lips glossy and pink. Other than that she wears no makeup. Her hair's braided down the side under a grey hat with a thick knitted band. Her bangs are tucked in making her eyes that much bluer against her pale skin. I scan her body. I like how she fills out her jeans and off the shoulder sweater in all the right places. Her belt cinches the wool sweater at her waist and she holds a long coat in her arms.

When my eyes reach hers again, her cheeks are flushed and she won't look directly at me. She's nervous and is biting at her shiny bottom lip. Suddenly, I want that lip in my mouth. The feeling startles me, and I have to push down the thoughts that start to pop into my head.

We're friends. Just friends.

"So we're going to a get together tonight," I say casually and open the door for her. Her blue eyes hold mine and I can hear her breathing speed up.

"What does that mean?"

I laugh. She totally doesn't trust me. Not

that I blame her. "It's small, so no need to hyperventilate."

Talia glares.

Shit. I forgot about the anxiety thing.

I walk around to the driver side and as I get closer my heart starts to beat faster. I have no idea why I'm taking her with me. I have no idea why I want her to be there with me.

But it feels right for her to be with me. I feel like she'll understand. But I'm still nervous. No, not nervous. Terrified.

Why am I dragging her into this? I can't even do right by Gram.

~

"So you never told me what you meant by get together?" Talia asks as she turns, watching me drive. My heart pounds, I'm making a mistake. Why would I ever think she would be okay with this?

"You'll see."

She opens her mouth to say something so I reach over and pat her leg. I snatch my hand back. What a grandma thing to do.

"You'll see when we get there. Tell me a story or something. We have a few minutes to kill."

I look at her fully this time. She is definitely attractive. Her thick arched eyebrows are scrunched together. I'm guessing she's deciding whether to push me or not. I grip the steering wheel tighter. I'm flip-flopping between excitement, dread and guilt. I still don't know why I am bringing her. Hell, I don't know why I need to do this in the first place.

"Tell you a story about what?" she asks.

I relax a little and smile at her.

"About you, Hat Girl. About how you became Hat Girl."

"I didn't realize I had become Hat Girl." She says it so seriously that I laugh. Loudly.

"Oh come on, Talia. Everyone at school calls you Hat Girl. I actually got ambushed today by a trio of hairspray and glitter asking if I could get them one of your hats."

She frowns and I laugh again.

"Seriously? You didn't know that. Wow, you really do live under a rock."

"Who said I live under a rock?" She crosses her arms. I'm pissing her off and I like it. Although I'm not sure why she chooses that to be the most offensive thing I've ever said.

"I did."

"Well, I don't."

"Ha! When's the last time you left your house?"

She opens her mouth again but I cut her off.

"With someone who wasn't 100 years

old... or to visit your grandma?"

Her glare deepens and her chest rises and falls rapidly.

"I, I, I don't have to defend myself to you. To you of all people."

"What's that supposed to mean?" It isn't fun now that she is turning it around on me. The twitch in my jaw starts.

"You come from a different world than me, Lachlan."

She's never said my name before and it makes my skin tingle.

"You and your tough guy crap. Just because I don't go out and party and do drugs and screw people doesn't mean I don't have fun."

I'm taken aback. Is that what she thinks of me? I glare at the road and for a brief moment. I feel ashamed. Ashamed of my reputation, of my lifestyle, of myself. But I don't do those things any more. She needs to know that. I need her know that but I have no idea why.

"Is that what you think I do?" I force a glare at her and she shrinks into the car seat. Her eyes are so wide, so big I feel I could crawl into them. I kind of want to.

She nods slowly. I clench my jaw tighter and fight back the slew of curse words that are always my first response.

I reposition my hands on the steering wheel and stare straight ahead. The sunlight glares off the road and I squint.

We drive in silence until I stop the car in front of a little church. I can feel Talia staring at me. When I look at her I'm prepared for a fight. I'm always prepared for a fight.

"I'm sorry I said that. It wasn't fair," she says.

I nod. That's not what I was expecting. She plays with the hem of her sweater.

"I should know what it's like for people like us," she continues.

Us?

"What do you mean people like us?"

She blushes and I want to touch her face.

Shit, I do like this girl. This is bad.

"I just mean that people don't know what really goes on," she points to her head, "in here, you know?"

I nod again. I'm afraid if I open my mouth I'll tell her everything. I want to tell her about him, the tattoos, the scars, the memories. I guess in about five minutes she's going to know some of it. Showing her will be easier than telling her.

My stomach jumps. In five minutes she's going to know things about me I've spent the last two years burying so deep that no one could find them.

For some crazy, fucked up and completely unknown reason, I feel like this is the right thing to do.

Talia glances out the window then back at me. She seems confused but I can see the curiosity there too. There has to be adventure lurking somewhere deep in Talia Gregory and I've decided I'm going to find it.

"Um, Lachlan? Why are we at a church?"

I grin at her. "Church is the best place for a first date. Isn't it?"

CHAPTER ELEVEN

Talia

I'm not sure if I should laugh. The look on his face says he's joking but after one more glance out the window I'm positive we're parked in front of a church.

"What's going on, Lachlan?" I ask. I have a feeling this means something to him. He goes pale every time I ask him what 'get together' means. He refuses to answer and the way he's so casually leaning against the car seat, his shoulders hunched and his arm thrown lazily across the back of my seat tell me this place means something to him. I decided after the diner and the Knitting Club meeting that the more relaxed Lachlan seems, the more uptight he actually feels.

If I'm right, and something serious is happening, then I have no idea why he would want to bring me along.

He watches me carefully, his eyes burning with intensity but the rest of him is casual.

"It's my birthday in a couple months," he says.

"Oh?" I shift in my seat, suddenly uncomfortable. "Happy birthday."

He chuckles and my face heats up. What was I supposed to say?

"Which means I'll be 18. I'm done with probation." He's still watching me. Searching for something. His arms cross in front of his chest, pulling his T-shirt tighter over his shoulders.

I wonder what he's protecting himself from. Everyone knows he's been to Juvie.

"Congratulations." I smile at him and his eyebrows furrow, which makes the smile fall from my face.

"That's a good thing, isn't it?" I ask.

He nods.

What is this guy about?

"Why are you looking at me like that?" I cross my arms this time.

His face quickly softens and that real authentic Lachlan, the one I'm starting to like shows up.

He clears his throat.

"I, uh, I still have to go to support meetings though. I thought maybe you'd come with me. The woman who runs it is always on me that I don't have anyone my own age-"

It's really strange seeing him like this.

Suddenly he's not looking at me. Scratching his elbow nervously. Cracking his knuckles.

"Your own age?"

"Yeah, anyone who's a friend that isn't part of, uh, my past life."

My heart sinks when he says friend. Why am I upset about that?

"Of course I'll come with you." I have about a million questions about this 'support meeting' but I restrain myself.

I can't just pounce on him for information. He isn't Janna, I think and there is a shot of pain that sparks in my chest at the thought of her.

"I know I didn't really give you a choice or anything. But you said that day after the diner that you couldn't help me if I didn't tell you."

He scratches the back of his neck. My limbs go all soft and fluttery and my stomach feels like it's floating. I don't know why I feel like this is such a huge deal, but I think for him it is. That crack in his facade I saw after the motorbike ride has opened up again. His face is tight and his eyes are wide. I feel like he's trying to see inside me.

"Tell me what?" I speak softly, trying to encourage him, not startle him out of finishing this confession.

"Well, I have a hard time talking about

119

shit, you know?"

Obviously.

"So I thought I'd bring you here. You'll figure it out faster than I can tell you. I'm pretty fucked up, Hat Girl. I just want you to know that."

I sit back, unaware that I had been leaning forward more and more with each of his words.

"Do you really have to swear so much?" I don't mean for these words to be my first, but this is what comes out.

He laughs again, relaxing back into his seemingly confident self. He cuts the engine to the car and then puts his hand on my shoulder. It sends a tingle down my arm where his thumb touches the skin of my collarbone.

"If my *swearing* is what concerns you the most about everything I've just said then I think you'll be just fine in there." He nods toward the church and squeezes my shoulder.

~

Lachlan's standing in front of the large wooden doors, his hand on the knob, but he won't open it. I'm just about to ask what's wrong when he turns to me with a expression of apprehension.

"I've never wanted to bring anyone here

before. But I just feel like you'll get it."

His face scrunches up as if he's thinking about what he just said and isn't happy about it. He swings open the door and gestures for me to go in first. I watch him as I walk past but whatever was just there, whatever emotion he was trying to suppress is gone.

He places his hand on the small of my back and lightly guides me through the warm church foyer to another set of doors. His touch makes me forget what he was just saying, and I just watch his face as we move to the next room. The way he takes in everything as if it were the only thing makes me shiver, especially when he directs that intense gaze my way.

"You okay?" he asks. His hand is still on that curve where my back slopes out to connect with my butt.

I nod because I don't trust my voice. A support meeting. Support for what? Why did I not think of this before? Why would he bring me here? Why me? Why now?

I snap my wrist a couple times before I feel a hand on my face. My mind spins and I can't focus. Breath on my ear.

That tune. I blink and he's stroking my cheek, still humming. How does he do that? He snaps me out of it faster than Nan.

"I'm sorry, Talia. I shouldn't have brought

you."

I shake my head.

"I'm fine," I say more for myself then him. "Really. I'm fine. I want to come with you."

More like I want to find out your story. Why you have this effect on me.

I force a smile.

"You sure?"

I nod again. He slides his hand from my cheek to my neck, over my shoulder and down my arm until my hand in firmly gripped in his. I'm so aware of the heat of his skin, the tingle that trails his touch, the electricity that crackles around me. He squeezes my fingers and I wonder if he feels the same thing.

Lachlan pushes open the door and pulls me through, dropping my hand when we get to the other side.

The space is a small conference room and it smells like a church, old paper, candle smoke and dusty carpet. I don't even remember the last time I was in a church but the smell is one that will stay with me forever. Like the wool shop. And Nan.

In the center of the room there's a circle of chairs set up with a few people already seated. It reminds me of the wool shop and how we sit and knit in a circle. This makes me feel a lot better.

Lachlan nudges me with his shoulder and leans toward me.

"Let the fun begin." he smiles and gestures to a seat in the back of the room.

His face goes pale and I follow his gaze to a tall blonde leaning against the back wall. He knows her. His face says it all. By the way he takes her in with that intense gaze, he knows her very well.

His back straightens and he walks stiffly over to her. She's way skinnier than me. And taller. And everything that I am not. I watch Lachlan as he leans into her and says something in her ear. She touches his face and my stomach sinks. I don't know why because it's not like anything could ever happen. Between us, I mean.

Lachlan ducks out from under her hand and steps back. He grabs her upper arm just under the armpit and storms past leaving me behind.

"I can't believe you, Violet." I hear Lachlan hiss.

"But Lannie, I needed to see you. I wanted to say congratulations. Lannie, you know I lo-"

The door slams out her words. Everyone in the small room turns to look at me.

I go into panic mode. I'm not sure if I should follow them. I'm not sure what they were fighting about and I'm definitely not sure I liked the way he pulled her out of the room like that.

I hesitate then take a step forward, then stop and take a step back.

Someone puts a hand on my shoulder and I spin around. A young woman is looking at me with her head cocked to one side and her long auburn hair hanging loose around her thin face. She's wearing a casual three-piece suit and the way she stands with such authority tells me she runs this group.

"Excuse me," she says softly. "I didn't mean to startle you."

"No, it's fine."

"I've never seen you before. I'm Samantha Turner. You are?"

"Talia," I say and awkwardly shake her hand. "Talia Gregory. I'm here with Lachlan."

I point to the door. "I mean, I was here with Lachlan."

The woman's eyebrows knit together in thought before she smiles.

"Lachlan's never brought anyone to Support before. This is a good thing. I'm so glad you're here, Talia."

If he's never brought anyone before then who is this Violet?

Samantha must sense it because she wraps her arm around my shoulder and guides me to the back of the room where she offers me a seat.

"That girl, Violet," she starts and then pauses to think. "Violet comes by every once in awhile but she is from Lachlan's past. She's a trigger. He knows that. I know that. So we try to keep her out of here. She doesn't seem to care much for the rules. I've never seen him this upset by it before. You must have something to do with that."

Samantha lifts her eyebrows while mine sink deeper into my forehead.

"A trigger for what?" I ask.

She laughs quietly to herself.

"He didn't tell you did he?" She shakes her head at the same time I do.

"No he didn't. He said I'd learn more about what he wanted to tell me by coming than by him telling me."

She laughs again.

"That sounds like something Lachlan would say. He isn't great with words. Believe me, I have spent two years trying to get him to open up about his addictions. To this day he refuses to talk about it beyond acknowledging it's existence."

"Addictions?" My heart skips a beat.

"Yes, this is a support group for Youth Addictions and Lachlan was ordered here by the court when he was arrested two years ago for trafficking."

I'm shocked that I'm not overly surprised and even more-so that I'm not panicking about it.

"Is he still doing drugs?" I ask. Not that she would know.

"I don't think so. I think that Grandmother of his keeps him in toe."

I smile. "Georgina's pretty awesome."

"You know her?"

I suddenly feel like I'm being interviewed, and I shift a little in my seat.

"Yeah, that's how I know Lachlan. Our grandma's are friends."

Samantha's face relaxes into relief.

"Good. I'm glad he has someone outside of his old group to go to. He doesn't have any friends outside of the drugs. It's always been what concerned me the most. I'm thrilled that he brought you along, even if it didn't go as I had hoped. It's progress to know he has someone like you to help him."

Her words feel like a thousand pounds. I feel pressure now. I feel like I have to help him or he could relapse or something. I know it's stupid but I can't stop my brain from thinking stupid things.

"Um, thanks." I stand up and Samantha grabs my wrist.

"It says a lot that he brought you here

today, Talia. Remember that when he's being... difficult... okay? He isn't quite sure what he wants yet."

It also says a lot that he just left me behind to deal with Violet. The girl who I'm *sure* said she loved him.

CHAPTER TWELVE

Lachlan

I'm on my way back into the church. I managed to get Violet to leave. She was high. She claimed she wasn't but I know better. I am so fucking familiar with the excuses. I wish she'd just stop. Or leave me out of it. Does that make me the biggest selfish asshole ever? No the fact that I left Talia inside is what makes me the biggest selfish asshole ever.

I should have told her.

Talia pushes open the door. Her dark braid pokes out of her grey beanie and glows in the orange overhead lights.

She walks right up to me so her sneakers are touching mine. She is taller than I originally thought. Or maybe she is just standing up straighter.

"You should have told me," she says. I can't tell if she's mad.

I cross my arms and lean back. It wasn't meant as a defensive thing but the way her face bends into a scowl tells me she is taking it as a defensive thing.

She grabs my forearms and pries them apart.

"Don't you go all cool guy on me now."

She points behind her toward the door, "What was that?"

I try to cross my arms again but she grabs my wrists. I've never had a girl manhandle me like Talia, first with her slapping me after the motorbike and now with the forcing my arms apart. I can easily stop her, I could pry her fingers off me without even trying. But I don't. I don't want to.

I get caught in her crazy blue eyes and something within me stops. Stops trying. Stops hiding. Her hands around my wrists feel amazing. The warmth that travels the length of me reminds me of when she had her arms around me on my motorbike and stroking her cheek during her panic attack and the buzz of electricity I felt when I was holding her hand earlier. One touch from this girl and I'm done. One look and I want to take down the wall I so carefully built to keep people out. A look that sees through me, like only Gram's can.

"She always does that." Violet, I mean. My voice is like a whisper and I drop my head to watch Talia's hands still curved around my arms.

"So that gives you the right to haul her around like that?" Her voice is high and it cracks. She's judging me. I can hear it in her voice and it shatters the warmth I felt moments before.

"You wouldn't understand," I mutter and step forward, forcing her to step away from me. She stumbles backwards and stares, open-mouthed. I turn and go to the driver door.

"You *are* a jerk, Lachlan McCreedy." Talia speaks evenly, calmly, but I can hear her breathing speed up. My whole body tenses.

"You act like such a tough guy. You think you're hiding behind your reputation but you really are just a jerk."

I turn slowly and take three long steps toward her. She flinches but she never looks away.

"What did you say?" I ask, but I heard her. She's right and I don't know how to deal with it.

"You heard me. And yes, I don't understand because you're too busy being a jerk to talk about it."

She steps closer to me and I'm overtaken by the urge to kiss her but my anger keeps me stubborn. My anger always controls me.

"Why did you bring me here, Lachlan?

Why did you want me to come here if you're just going to leave me behind? You've obviously figured out that I have a hard time with this kind of stuff? Why here?"

I open my mouth but my jaw sticks. Even if I wanted to say something, anything, I can't make myself do it.

Because I feel something for you I've never felt before. Because I want to talk to you. Because I want you to know. Because I want you.

"Am I just a game to you? The quiet crazy girl that you want to challenge yourself with? See if you can destroy my life so you can hang my card on your collection? Well get in line, buddy, because you're not the first."

This time my mouth closes. Still no words. It shatters me to think she thinks this of me. I know what most people have to say about me, but she is different. This is Talia.

Talia's glare softens but the fire I'd never seen before still blazes in her eyes.

"Take me home."

She gets in the car, slamming the door. The sound pulls me out of my trance and I move around to the driver side, closing the door softly. How did this get so intense so quickly?

Right, I'm a jerk.

Just like that my fight is gone. I want her to know. But no one knows. No one but me and

Gram and mom. And *him,* of course.

I sigh loudly and she faces me, eyes narrowed and arms crossed, but she's shaking. Sticking my tattoo covered arm out to her, I pull up the sleeve of my T-shirt to expose my shoulder. The tattoos go onto my back but she'll get the point.

Her lip trembles as she looks from me to my arm and back again.

"Go ahead, touch them." I flick the interior light on and we are bathed in the harsh white light.

She just holds my gaze until I reach out and take her hand. I press her fingers to my skin and tingles shoot up my arm, hitting me right in the chest. She's going to turn me into one of those guys. One of those guys who blubber about their feelings and that terrifies me, but for now I continue to press her fingers into my skin.

At first she seems scared, her hand rigid and pulling away, but then she feels it. I can tell by the way her expression changes from fear to shock.

"Is that a..."

"Scar? Yes." She begins to move her fingers on her own, traveling up my forearm until she finds another one. Her eyes get wider but she never takes them off me.

"But how?" She sounds terrified. She

doesn't believe it.

"Because he said I deserved it." I start to pull my arm back and she grips me tighter pulling my arm so hard I have to lean across the console. She puts my arm in her lap and runs both her hands up and down it. The sensation is tormenting me, the mixture of desire for her to keep going and the pain of the memories those scars hold is too much.

"Your dad?" She's starting to get it.

I nod and her eyes glaze over. I wait for the pity but it doesn't come.

"There are so many," she whispers to herself just as her fingers grazed the top of my wrist band. My heart punches me in the chest from the inside. My ribs feel as if they will crack. *I need this,* I tell myself. I need to let someone in.

I shake, for the first time in years, I shake. Talia takes the clasp in her fingers. She doesn't say anything but just licks her bottom lip before biting it. I nod slowly but I have to look away. I can't watch her. I want her to know, but I don't. My brain is such a fucking mess that I close my eyes and lean back against the headrest.

I hear the snap of the band's catch.

Talia drops my arm and my heart falls with it. There's no turning back now.

She gasps.

"Lachlan!"

She wraps her hand around my wrist and presses her palm onto the long scar. I finally get the guts to look at her and swivel my head without lifting it off the headrest.

As soon as my eyes meet hers she flings herself across the car and I catch her as she wraps her arms around me. I bury my face in her neck, which is not something I would normally do, but she smells like vanilla and almonds and I can't help it.

She hugs me tight and whispers in my ear, "I do get it, Lachlan. I know what it feels like to have nowhere to hide from yourself. To feel like you have no escape. I get it."

My shoulders tense and she pulls back. Those eyes. She does get it. I see understanding, not pity, behind the flecks of ocean blue.

And it scares the shit out of me.

CHAPTER THIRTEEN

Talia

Nan's saying something to me, I can hear her voice but I'm not paying attention. I'm thinking about Lachlan. I have been all week. Mostly about his scars, specifically the long thin bump that ran along the inside of his wrist. He wouldn't tell me if it was his fathers doing or his own. Actually, he never said anything after I saw it. He put on his band and drove me home. And he hasn't spoken to me since. He ditched out on our last meeting and I had to go see the director of the Christmas Charity drive by myself.

"Tali, darling? Are you okay?" Nan reaches down to the end of the couch, where I'm sitting and pats my knee. I try to smile at her but I can't. She looks terrible. I've stopped asking about it because all she ever says is "I'm fine, darling." Which is garbage because she's losing weight, her skin is no longer luminescent but grey and sallow. Her eyes don't shine like they did, and I can tell it is taking her a lot of effort to move around.

"Sorry Nan. I was just lost." I lift the half-done hat, trying to suggest that's what I was lost in. Nan doesn't fall for it. She purses her lips and I sigh. Busted.

"I can't talk about it, Nan. It's not mine to talk about."

"Is it about that boy?"

She's good.

"Yeah, I'm struggling with this planning thing. He's making it worse. He's supposed to help but he spends most of his time sneaking around and missing meetings and kidnapping me." I intentionally leave out the part where I feel like I'll disintegrate every time he's close enough to touch.

Nan's eyes widen. "What do you mean kidnapping you?"

"Not literally. He just always wants to take me to these places that make me uncomfortable. I'm not his type. I don't get what he wants with me."

Nan's shock settles into a smile and she scoots to my end of the couch so our knees are touching. The movement seems like it hurts her and she coughs a dry painful sounding cough. I rub her back until she stops.

"Are you sure you're okay, Nan? This has

been getting worse for weeks. Shouldn't you go to the doctor or something?" My voice is pleading and whiny but she pats my face lightly.

"I'm fine, darling."

I roll my eyes.

"Maybe this boy likes you," she continues, "but doesn't know how to deal with it. From what I know of him, he's had a very poor up bringing. He hasn't had many positive experiences in his life."

"Well it doesn't give him the right to be a jerk." I'm not really arguing. I know it must have been hard for him.

"No, you're right. It doesn't. But you have to be understanding if you like him back. He deserves a certain amount of leeway. Unless he's cruel, or violent to you then you stay away from him, okay?"

My jaw hangs open while I try to think of what to say.

"I, uh, he's not violent." Which isn't entirely true. I did watch him walk Violet out of the church so fast her feet barely touched the ground. But I also slapped him in the face while having a panic attack, so I'm not sure *I'm* not the violent one. "And I don't like him. Not like that. We're... we're just friends."

Which also isn't entirely true. I remember what it feels like to run my hands along his bare skin, to have his cheek press against mine, and to hold him on his bike. Every time I touch him it feels like more than just friends. It shouldn't.

Nan raises an eyebrow at me. I know I'm not fooling her but I refuse to say it out loud.

"Have you talked to him? Have you asked him what he wants with you?"

My cheeks burn. "No way." Again, not true. But I guess I didn't ask, I just accused him of using me.

"Well you can't be angry at him for not telling you if you aren't willing to ask."

Unable to think fast enough to form words, I just sigh and go back to my knitting. I'm not sure I really want to know. Everything with Deacon hasn't helped my faith in starting a relationship. Not that Lachlan does relationships anyway.

I feel Nan's self-satisfied gaze on me as I continue to knit my next hat. The hat that is quickly making me one of the most noticed people at school, which is just one more thing that makes me uncomfortable. I pride myself on being invisible but it's getting harder with the hats and Lachlan and I've even heard whispers about Janna and me. I've had nine panic attacks since the night Lachlan took me to his meeting, nine, and it's only been a few days.

The door swings open and my mother comes in the back door. In her hands she holds a tray of coffees and a bag. My father isn't with her. She's dressed like she's going to a cocktail party, in a short red dress, and her high heeled peep toes click on the hardwood floor as she makes her way to us.

Doesn't she know it's cold outside? It's almost October.

She bends quickly and kisses the side of my head before setting down her stuff on the coffee table. She's pale, but her make up is perfect, as usual.

Nan holds out her arms and mom gives her a quick hug. Mom isn't one for physical attention, one thing she didn't get from Nan. Nan likes to hug for inappropriate amounts of time, not that I mind. But other people do.

"Hey, Mom. Sweetie." My mom looks from Nan to me. I smile and go back to knitting.

"So nice of you to visit, Mitts." Nan says to my mom and she blushes. I still don't know why Nan calls her Mitts, but Mom and I never talk and Nan says it's Mom's story to tell.

"How are you feeling? Are you ready? Are you comfortable? It's so cold in here. I'm going to turn up the heat."

Nan takes hold of Mom's wrist and pats her hand.

"Ready for what?" I ask, watching them

intently. They both look at me then back at each other. Exchanging a glance of secrecy.

"I'm fine, dear. Really. And I am ready."

"Ready for what?" I ask again.

"You should really tell her," Mom says with a sadness in her eyes I've never seen before.

Those words set off a massive string of worst case scenario visions in my head. I block out everything and the thoughts tumble so fast I don't even realize I've stopped breathing. I feel warm hands on my face and Nan's nose against mine. I find her eyes with mine and suck in a ragged gulp of air so fast I start to cough.

Mom stands over Nan's shoulder her face fixed in defiance.

"This is why I want her back on medication. This method of yours isn't working," she says. That has my attention. I'd rather die than take that stuff again. It makes me feel like I'm dead, a constant state of I-couldn't-care-less.

"No you're not, she's doing very well. Give it time, Mitts."

Like a curtain slides open behind my eyes, I'm suddenly focused.

"Tell me what, Nan? What's wrong?" I demand.

Nan slides back down to the end of the

couch and I see my mother roll her eyes behind her and she plops down on the armchair.

"You baby her. She needs to toughen up. Stop treating her like a child." Mom hisses at her.

Nan frowns at mom. "She *is* a child."

I disagree with both of them, so I have no idea what to do with the attitude that's boiling inside of me. I want to tell them both off. I've never wanted to tell off Nan before.

Nan grips my hands and I focus on her, blocking out Mom.

"I have Cancer, darling. I'm so sorry I didn't tell you sooner, but I wanted to be certain."

She has concern in her eyes as she watches me, as if she's preparing to have to pick me up off the floor. I'm confused.

Cancer. No one I know has ever had cancer.

"What kind of cancer?"

"My lungs. I will be starting treatment next week." She squeezes my hand harder.

My head is swimming.

"But what if you-" I can't say it. The treatment might not work. She'll get sick. Really sick.

Nan pulls me to her just as the first tears well in my eyes.

"Why didn't you tell me? Why did you keep this from me? You could–What if you–" I sob into her chest.

"Die?" she finishes for me and I cry harder.

How can she do this to me? Doesn't she know how much I need her?

"It's not that definitive, darling. Yes, I might not be able to survive but the doctor thinks we caught it at a decent time. I'm healthy, and I'm old, but not that old. There's also a chance I might live," Nan coos, running her hand through my hair. She's trying to make it sound better. I push back so I can see her through my tears. She is wearing a small smile but it's pasted on. Mom has moved to sit beside me and rubs my back lightly. Mom never touches me like this. It has to be serious.

I suddenly want the pills again. Then I wouldn't feel this. My mind tumbles with thoughts and Nan dies in every one of my scenarios. My brain isn't wired for happy. I can't control it anymore.

"But," is all I manage before the breakdown happens. The next sound that comes from my throat is a sound that would embarrass me on any other day. The tears flow freely and I cling to my grandmother as if she were already dead. I vaguely feel my mother pat my back one last time and mutter to Nan that it was probably a mistake to tell me.

It takes me a long time to calm down. I don't have a panic attack though, I'm too broken to panic.

"Do you want to talk about it? Do you want to know about the treatments?" Nan asks after a long and painful silence where I just stare at my hands. My hat is soaked in tears. I'll have to make another one.

I shake my head. How is she so calm about this? How can she just sit there and talk about it like it's no big deal?

I stand and shove my things into my bag a little more forcefully than necessary. Waves of emotion are overtaking my body. Drowning me in fear, sorrow, anger, fear, sorrow, anger. I can't feel one long enough to grab hold of it. All I can do is try to stay above it, try to breathe.

I throw the bag over my shoulder and leave the room. For the first time in my life I leave Nan without saying goodbye. For the first time in my life I'm angry with her.

~

My body's numb against the cold air as I pedal my bike. When I stop I'm not at my house. I can't remember when I decided to change the route. I throw my bike down on the small front lawn and don't even bother walking on the path. I don't even bother walking at all. I run, sliding to a stop just in front of the door.

Why am I here?

My finger presses the doorbell.

Because I have nowhere else to go.

I stand cold and shaking on the front step.

He opens the door. As soon as I see him a fresh river of tears bubbles up behind my eyelids and spills down my cheeks.

"I didn't know where else to go," I sob as Lachlan stares wide-eyed. "I have no one."

CHAPTER FOURTEEN

Lachlan

I stumble backwards as Talia's body crashes into mine. I have to support her weight as well as my own. My arms instinctively wrap around her but my brain has stalled. Ten seconds ago I was watching TV, and now I'm holding a sobbing girl. A girl I've been avoiding for her own protection. A girl who's better off without me, but seems to always end up in my arms anyway.

"Hey, hey, what's wrong?" I reach up and entwine my fingers in her hair. This is not a natural movement for me, but with Talia it feels right, safe. She pulls back.

Her eyes are huge, red, and puffy. She can't talk between the hiccups, or if she is talking I don't pick up a single word.

I pull her close and step back into the house so I can shut the door. She lets me guide her to the living room and lower her onto the couch. She practically sits on top of me, her arms still like a vice around my neck.

I'm trying to piece things together but I've never understood crying girls. She could have bumped her elbow or someone could have died. They react the same way to everything.

I feel her tears soak through my T-shirt and I'm momentarily grossed out that she's probably snotted all over me. I sit still for what seems like hours, stealing glances over my shoulder at the TV. I can't do anything until she tells me what's wrong. Finally her breathing slows and I risk asking her again.

"Talia," I start cautiously. "What happened?"

She pulls back sharply and the tears fill her eyes again. Her skin is soaking wet and she wipes her nose with the sleeve of her sweater.

"She has cancer. She has–" The words get stuck in her throat and come out as a gurgle. "How could she not tell me? She's, she's gunna die, Lachlan."

My chest constricts painfully. I can't imagine. I thought back to when Gram fell in the shower and how scared I was. I reach for her and she sobs again.

"She's gunna die, and then I really will have no one."

She flings her arms around me again and this time I scoop her up onto my lap and press her as tight as I can into me. I burrow my face into her hair and rub her back.

I can't fix this, I can't help her and I ache for her. I understand her, but people hate being told that. People survive Cancer all the time, too. I already know not to say that either. I wish I had *something* to say as she nuzzles closer in my neck, her tears soaking my collar. But words aren't really my thing.

All I can think of is to hold on tighter, to try and absorb her pain. I know it's impossible, but I want to try.

I start to hum Gram's song. It worked before. Maybe it'll work now.

~

I gently shake Talia's shoulder. She cried herself to sleep on my lap. Now she's snoring on the couch, completely plugged up from leaking every ounce of moisture from her body. She stirs lightly and turns her head to look at me. A smile plays on her lips, but there's sadness in her eyes.

"I'm so sorry, Lachlan. I shouldn't have come. I'm so sorry."

She tries to sit up but I press my hand against her shoulder and shush her.

"Don't be ridiculous, Hat Girl. I love crying girls showing up on my doorstep. It's super sexy." I try to lighten the mood by pulling half my mouth up into the arrogant smile I know she hates.

"Oh, God." She covers her face with her hands and groans. "I bet I look hideous."

I grab her wrists and pull them from her face.

"I'm not going to respond to that. I feel like I'll get in trouble no matter what I say."

She smiles wider and turns her head, hiding it in the pillow.

I let her go and stand.

"I have to go get Gram from her card game."

Talia sits up quickly and then clutches her head and lays back down.

"You're welcome to stay here. Rest. I put some headache pills and water on the coffee table."

"I should go." She tries to get up again.

"Really, Talia. Stay, please. I want you to."

Her mouth pulls up at the corners again. I'm beginning to look forward to that smile. Waiting for it to appear.

~

I don't tell Gram Talia's at the house. When we get home and there's a sleeping girl on the couch, her eyebrows rise but she doesn't say anything. Gram's outspoken but she's also a behind the scenes gal. She doesn't like public disturbances.

"It's Talia, Gram. She got some bad news

about her grandmother. She came to see you." I add the last part in because I don't want Gram to know she had straddled me on the couch and soaked me with tears because she had no one else. Gram's understanding but I'm 'still in high school' and she doesn't like boy-girl-funny-business, as she calls it, in her house. A rule I've always respected, mostly because Violet preferred gas station bathrooms, park benches, back alleys and anywhere else we could have been caught by actual authorities.

Gram clutches her hands together and quickly makes her way to the couch. Talia lifts her arm off her face and yawns, her shirt has ridden up and a strip of milky skin that stretches over her hipbone catches my eye. She sits up without a word and wraps her arms around Gram who strokes her back. I lean against the wall trying to think of when such little skin could cause such a stir within me.

~

"So when does she start treatment?" Gram asks while blowing on her tea.

I look between them, not saying anything, just watching. Gram gave Talia some knitting needles and she's already half done a scarf. It seems to calm her down. I smile to myself. She cares too much about everything and I don't care enough.

"Next week," Talia says. "I feel so bad Georgina. I just left. Nan's sick and I'm worried about my own feelings. How awful is that?"

Tears fill her eyes again, and I'm just about to lean over but Gram beats me to it. She clutches Talia's knee with her arthritic hand, which makes Talia smile.

"Florence understands, dear. It's not awful. You love her very much, your feelings are very valid."

Gram leans back and continues to blow on her tea. We sit in silence for a while before Gram stands and slaps her thighs.

"Well this old lady has to take her buns to bed," she says. "Lachlan, you won't stay up too late? You have school in the morning." It's not as much of a question as it sounds so I just nod.

Talia stands to hug Gram then turns to me.

"I should go. My parents are probably worried about me."

I swear she rolls her eyes when she says it, but they are so red and puffy I might be seeing things.

"I'll walk you out." I stand and stretch quickly before placing my hand on her shoulder and guiding her to the door. *She's so fragile,* I think.

With Talia I am in completely new territory. She's completely opposite of what I'm used to.

~

We stand on the porch and Talia says for the thousandth time that she would rather ride her bike than have me drive her.

"It's not a big deal, your bike would fit in the Granny wagon."

Talia laughs and I beam. So lame. She *is* going to turn me into one of those guys.

She puts her hands on my upper arms and cocks her head to one side.

"I'm fine, Lachlan. Really. Thank you. For the offer and...for everything else."

She casts her eyes down to her sneakers and drops her hands. I reach out and cup the back of her neck with one hand and push her bangs off her forehead with the other. I pull her in and kiss her right on her hair line. Vanilla and almonds with a hint of tears. I squeeze her into my chest and she holds onto my waist. I kiss her forehead again and slide her away from me. It's more of a friend gesture, but if I kiss her how I really want too. Why do I want to kiss her this bad?

"Take care of yourself, Hat Girl. You're stronger than you think."

She smiles and runs her fingers down my arm, the one with the scars. This doesn't feel like a friend gesture, but I'm probably reading into it.

"So are you."

She turns and leaves. Even when she's out of sight I still stand on the porch with my arm tingling.

CHAPTER FIFTEEN

Talia

It's the first weekend in October and the day I have to submit my work for jurying. It's also Nan's first treatment. I've been avoiding everyone. Not unusual for me. My mom, Nan, Georgina. I even missed the last Knitting Club meeting. I've especially been avoiding Lachlan.

Did I say avoid? I mean I run away every time I see him but he texts me constantly and I always text back. I can't help myself. I want to be friends with him. I feel calm and comfortable around him now, which makes me uncomfortable. That doesn't even make sense.

Want me to come with u?

I stare at my phone too much now. I'm becoming one of those girls. I don't want to talk to him, but I don't want to not talk to him.

I sigh and text back.

Nah, I should go alone. I don't want you covered in my snot again. Lol

I blush and shove the phone into my bag. It beeps almost immediately and I snatch it up. Yup. Totally becoming one of those girls.

But there's nothing I like more than being covered in your snot. C U 2nite @ the shelter? Shitty...

My heart jumps. Volunteering. I forgot.

I start to text back. I rewrite the text so many times I'm sick of myself. I used to gag when Janna would ask me what she should say to a guy.

"Say whatever you want," I would always reply. My stomach drops and churns a few times. I wonder who coached her through hooking up with Deacon. I miss her but I'm angry with her. It's a weird space to be in.

I toss the phone back into the bag and tighten the scarf around my neck. The air is cold but the sun is warm. Leaves crunch under my bike tire and I wonder when I'll have to give up the bike for good and go back to bussing it.

I swing my leg over the bar and push forward in the direction of the hospital. I haven't apologized to Nan yet. I have to. I have to be there for her.

~

She's already hooked up to a machine

when I get to the hospital.

I pull up a chair and kiss her on the forehead. The nurse squints at me and I smile. I've already done a lot of begging to be in this room and don't want to mess it up.

"Nan, I just wanted to say," I start, pulling my chair closer. Nan raises her hand and stops me.

"It's fine, darling. I forget sometimes that you don't see death the same way I do."

My heart stops at the word death. What does she mean see it the same way? Death is death.

I start to form the question but Nan starts talking.

"I've lost all four of my grandparents, both my parents and my husband. I won't say I'm used to it, but I will say I understand it. I love you very much but your mother is right. You need to be aware, you need to be strong and I, unfortunately, have spent too much time protecting you and not enough preparing you."

I'm at a loss. My first instinct is to argue with her. Seeing her sitting in that chair attached to a tube that's feeding chemicals into her blood, I can't bring myself to argue.

Instead, I pull out the white hat I made for the jury. I had to start over since I cried all over the last one and then destroyed it in a mild outburst I had after getting back from Lachlan's and having my mother ground me. The first time that I needed to go out and she gets mad at me for it. I've just added it to the list of her strange behavior. Spending ridiculous amounts of time in the bathroom, staring at me but refusing to say anything and then getting really, really mad about something that should have been understandable. I almost wish she'd go back to avoiding me.

The new white hat has both red and green cables and I pinned a piece of holly on the side. It's pretty. Christmassy. Snowy. I knew Nan would love it. I still prefer the skull.

I place it in Nan's lap and watch as a huge smile spreads across her face.

"Sold," she says and throws it back to me.

"What do you mean sold? And you didn't even look at it." I'm offended and guessing it shows on my face by the way Nan's looking at me.

"I don't need to. It's perfect. And after it is juried and accepted, I want to buy it. I'm going to lose all my hair just in time for the snow, and I need something to keep my head warm."

I purse my lips, understanding her attempt at humor, but I don't think it's funny. I don't see how I can or will ever laugh at this. She's dying and she's making a joke out of it. Suddenly I'm angry all over again.

I stuff the hat back in my bag and start another hat while Nan hums. She's not as good as Georgina but her voice is still soothing.

I am half done another hat by the time Nan is ready to go.

"You're so talented," she says.

The hat is multicolored. That crazy yarn dyed ten different colors. I chuckle to myself while turning the hat in my hands.

"No wonder they call me Hat Girl," I say thinking of the boxes of hats I have in my room. It's only October and already I've made about 25 of them.

"Hat girl?" Nan asks.

"At school," I explain. "It's what they call me now ever since Lachlan started wearing my hat. Everyone wants one."

"That's wonderful," Nan smiles weakly. I have never described anything about Nan as being weak and it makes me hurt all over. It feels like she is one step closer to death. My foot taps and that tight feeling in my chest that screams panic is closing in.

I take a deep breath and try to remind myself that she is right in front of me. She's right here.

I lean forward and hug her. She pats my

face then we make our way to my parents car.

We drive in silence. Nan has her eyes closed and her head lolls to one side. Frail. I hate it. I hold back tears and stare at the road.

"Love you forever, Nan," I say when I drop her off.

"Forever and always," she whispers and climbs slowly from the car. I feel the sting of tears and need to get out of here.

~

I cinch my coat tighter around me and pull my scarf over my nose as I stand outside in the wind. Lachlan was supposed to be here 15 minutes ago. My one leg shakes and I shift my weight. I hate waiting. I cross my arms and groan. I'm mad. First because he's late and second because it seems I'm always mad at him and third because I'm stuck standing in the cold with nothing but thoughts of my disaster of a day.

Starting with Nan then moving on to dropping my hat off for jurying my day just kept getting worse. I forgot–no I pushed it out of my head–that the director of the Cozy Christmas Charity Drive was Deacon's grandmother who insisted on talking about my and Deacon's break-up. She isn't very cozy.

I forget that not all Nans are kind and caring and smell like baking like mine, or meddling and funny and old fashioned like Georgina. Greta is cold and calculated and really just an awful person.

I had a panic attack after I dropped off my white hat and she looked down her crooked pretentious nose at it and asked, "You're submitting this?" Then I came home and cried and now the jerk I may, or may not, have a crush on has stood me up for the only requirement of the Charity Drive, volunteering.

I just about write him off when I see Georgina's car turn a little too quickly onto my street. Lachlan is out of the car so fast that I wonder if he remembered to put it into park.

I glare.

"I know, I know. I'm an asshole. I'm sorry. I'm here." Lachlan wraps his arm around my shoulder and ushers me into the car. He closes the door for me before I can respond.

~

Lachlan has this strange mixture of mysterious bad boy with southern gentlemen with rockstar charm. I can't keep up with him and he has me spun around so many times it's hard to keep track of what I like about him and what I don't. Sometimes they overlap.

No, they always overlap.

I'm watching him as we fold towels in the shelter's basement laundry room. It's steamy and hot. The faint smell of fabric softener mixes with the thick, musty air and it's hard to breathe without tasting it.

Lachlan's sleeves are pushed up and his tattoos flex and stretch. It's like a mural, arranged in no particular order other than to flow from one to the other in a lucid and dreamlike swirl of color and shape. Most of the images are kind of dark and scary, but I think that has a lot to do with whatever his dad did to him. I try to pick out different elements but he moves so fast I can't focus on anything but that wristband. The wristband that covers the huge scar across his inner wrist.

"You never did tell me what that symbol meant." I lay a towel on top of the one he just folded and we both grab another one.

"I didn't."

He doesn't even look over at me and I seriously want to stomp my foot. How immature is that? But I can't help it. I roll my eyes instead.

"Are you ever going to?"

Lachlan places his folded towel down on the washer and flips around to face me. He leans on the machine and crosses one foot over the other.

Here we go, tough guy.

"Are you ever going to tell me why you're so rigid all the time?"

I step back both literally and metaphorically. "I am not rigid," I say, my voice hard. My body stiffens, which totally doesn't help my case. "And that's a very personal question."

"So is this." Lachlan holds out his arm.

I stumble over words that form in my mouth. I forget them as soon as they dissolve on my tongue. I have no idea how long we stand there with my jaw wobbling like one of the wind-up teeth toys that chatter.

Lachlan laughs, the arrogant one that slides it's way under my skin and leaves me both hot and cold. He stretches his arms up in the air and casually grips a thick solid looking water pipe that hangs from the low ceiling. He lifts himself up like a monkey and dangles in the air. I can see his stomach and the elastic band of his underwear and I try to look away. He sets himself down on the washer and not once has he shifted his eyes away from mine. He's making fun of me, but I can't figure out how, or why. I also don't know where this display of macho-male is coming from but it makes my stomach flutter.

"Tell me, Hat Girl." Lachlan's voice gets lower, huskier. "Have you ever done anything bad in your life? And I'm not talking, like, stole a candy bar as a kid, bad..."

My heart pounds and my breathing speeds up but this is definitely not a panic attack. This is totally different. Exciting.

"I mean really bad," he continues.

Lachlan spreads his knees apart and leans forward slightly, using the pipe just above his head to brace himself.

My jaw now feels like it's disappeared altogether and my cheeks fill with heat. I stutter over a few things that could constitute as bad but I stop myself because I know that's not what he means.

I take a step toward him, my feet moving without my permission.

"Bad?" I finally push out, but my voice squeaks. I am too flustered to be embarrassed.

His smile widens and his eyes darken behind his fringe of curls. I'm standing and staring like a total idiot surrounded by laundry, with nothing but the swishing sound of the washing machine to cut the tension.

"Like, I don't know, make out with the guy who has the worst Juvie record in town? In the basement of a homeless shelter? On a washing machine?" Lachlan says, raising one eyebrow.

I try to swallow, but I fail and a bubble of air gets stuck in my throat. I cough and Lachlan laughs again. I really want to be mad at him, for putting me on the spot like this, but as soon as the word 'make-out' comes out of his mouth I can't stop staring at his lips. Everything else forgotten.

"Come here, Hat Girl." He is still leaning forward, bracing himself on the pipe. I hesitate and then take a step.

This is such a bad idea.

"Clos-er." He drags out the last part. Definitely a really bad idea. I take another step. My sneakers are silent on the concrete floor because the step is slow and tentative. My steps are the only thing that's moving slowly though. My heart is racing, my legs are shaking, and my mind is spinning.

Why does he always do this?

He's pulling me toward him with his eyes, his lips, his crooked nose and perfect teeth. The way he leans forward, the way his fingers loosen and tighten their grip on the low hanging pipe, the way that he slides to the very edge of the washing machine, all tell me he is serious.

Is this how he picks up other girls?

I take another step. I'm standing in front of

him. I shouldn't be. Both sides of my brain are screaming so loud at the other I can't tell anymore. I want. I don't want. I desire. I fear. It all happens at once.

"A little closer," he whispers now. His knees spread even wider apart and I step in between them. He's leaning over me and I feel his breath on my face. My arms are locked at my side.

"We shouldn't, Lachlan." My head is angled down. My voice is breathy. It matches the light but also heavy feeling in my chest, my stomach, my knees. I feel like I'm floating and sinking at the same time.

"I know we shouldn't." He touches his forehead to mine. "But I want to. I have to. It's killing me."

I close my eyes, our foreheads still touching. My nose brushes against his. He leans further into me. I tilt up a little more and my lips touch his.

I brace myself on his knees so I don't fall. For a second I feel like I'll faint, which is stupid. I've kissed boys before.

But not this boy.

Lachlan eases off the washer, hanging from the pipe until his feet touch the floor but his lips never leave mine. He slides one arm around my waist and pulls me into him. Hard. He increases the pressure of the kiss and my lips part. His tongue just touches mine. I really do think I'm going to faint when suddenly he stops.

He pulls me into him again, pressing my head against his chest. I can feel and hear his heart beating faster than mine.

Is he nervous? No, Lachlan doesn't get nervous.

He clears his throat and everything in my body that was working at warp speed only a second ago stops. The feeling is like slamming into reverse going 100 miles an hour.

I peek over my shoulder toward the door to the basement. The director of the shelter is leaning against the doorway and doesn't look impressed.

"Sorry, sir. She was having an attack. Just calming her down." Lachlan's voice sounds normal but his chest heaves under my cheek with short breaths. My arms are still locked at my sides.

"Is she going to be okay?" The director sounds concerned but there's something skeptical in his voice too. He has been director for years, so he's seen my attacks and knows how Nan calms me down.

"I think so sir, thank you." There's the southern gentleman part, accent and all. The director doesn't leave right away so I wave behind me and will my voice to come out even.

"I'm fine. I just need a minute. Thank you."

As soon as the metal door clangs shut Lachlan relaxes back on the washer, taking me with him. He rests his chin on my head.

"Thanks. For covering," I whisper into his chest.

He hugs me tighter but doesn't say anything. It's silent for a minute. Just the swish of the washer.

"Forgiveness," he says abruptly.

This startles me and I try to pull back but I'm too wrapped up and he won't let me go.

"Huh?"

"The symbol. On the wristband. It means forgiveness."

My arms go around his waist and I relax into him.

"For him, or you?" I wonder out loud. His dad had abused him, but he had also turned to abuse, just a different form.

"Both," he doesn't hesitate. His voice is cold and distant.

We stand silent for a long time before he leans back to look at me with those absorbent brown eyes. He lifts my chin with his finger and kisses me lightly on the nose.

"Hat Girl, what have you done to me?"

CHAPTER SIXTEEN

Lachlan

I really don't know how I got here, but here I am nonetheless. Talia sits with me on Gram's front porch. She's one step down and sitting between my legs. I have my arms wrapped around her shoulders and she's leaning on me playing with my wristband. I'm slowly getting comfortable with her touching my wrist. I really like that she's not afraid to ask but never pushes.

It's probably why I'm sitting here with her now.

I'm not sure how a kiss in a damp basement turned into movie night at my place in a week, but like I said, here we are.

I don't think I've ever had a movie night with a girl.

"Lachlan?"

I jump at her voice.

"What? Sorry, wasn't listening."

"I said we have to set up a schedule for working the booth and decide on a theme for the Charity Drive, which means you have to come to the meeting tomorrow."

She glares when I groan and slaps my hand.

"I also have to do Math homework, a history paper and about a bazillion Chem labs if I hope to pass this semester. That doesn't mean I want to." I chuckle and turn her to face me.

She glares harder and I mock her, mimicking her movements until she smiles. I love that smile.

Whoa, like. I like that smile.

"You look like someone just slapped you in the face." Talia giggles. I've never heard her giggle.

I do the only thing I can think of. I lift her up so she is kneeling and we are face to face. I cup her face in my hand and kiss her. It's the second time we've kissed and it's just as crazy as the first. Like my reaction to a tiny strip of her skin, I'm confused by the way her lips feel against mine. I mean kissing is great, but these lips are greater.

That sounds fucked. I didn't know there could be a difference in lips. I've kissed a lot of girls. Some were good, some not so much. No one feels like Talia.

She wraps her arms around me, and I remember I'm kissing her. I deepen the kiss by tracing my tongue along her bottom lip and they part. As soon as our tongues meet I am instantly ready for a straight up home-run, right outta the park type advancement so I pull away. It's not easy.

Her breath catches and her cheeks are red. For a second I think it's cute how totally clueless she is, then I'm stabbed with guilt so intense that it makes me wince. She doesn't deserve to be dragged into my shit. She deserves to be with someone who is easy, happy... not quite as screwed up as me.

"Are you okay?" She sounds wary, like I'm going to tell her to do me or get off my porch.

I go to answer, but my cell phone buzzes. I slide it out of my pocket, look and slide it back in. When my eyes meet back up with Talia's her eyebrows are pulled together in disappointment.

"Are you ever going to tell me what those are about?" Talia points to my jeans pocket and a grin bubbles to the surface of my face.

Too easy.

"Maybe someday I'll show you what those are about. If you play your cards right."

I lean back and watch her face. Her eyebrows furrow in confusion and slowly as she starts to realize I wasn't talking about my phone her brows get higher and higher until her eyes are big ocean blue saucers. I laugh loudly. I shouldn't do that to her but I can't help myself.

"Why do you do that?"

"Because you make it too easy."

She frowns for a moment.

"No, I mean skirt around stuff like that. Why do you act like it doesn't matter? I've seen the way you look at that phone. I just wish you'd talk about it. If not with me then someone else."

The switch has been flipped. I don't want to be pissed, but I can't control it. I hate that anger is my go-to emotion.

"Because crying about your problems doesn't make them go away." I cross my arms. She stands and the hurt look is enough to crush the anger out of me. I didn't mean it like that. I didn't mean her.

"Low, Lachlan."

Talia turns and walked away before I have a chance to explain. Now instead of being mad at her, I'm mad at me.

I need to chill out. I run my hand through my hair until the curls are fuzzy and standing straight up.

I want to tell her. The whole story is on the tip of my tongue every time I'm around her. *Why can't I do it?*

My phone buzzes again, and I want to smash it. Be done with it. With the drugs, the

running, my past.
    Be done with myself.

CHAPTER SEVENTEEN

Talia

I don't cry as I walk home in the cold air. I'm too busy arguing with myself about whether it's a terrible idea to get involved with Lachlan. I knew he'd be too much, but there's something that draws me to him. Ever since the ride on the motorbike when he calmed me down. I just wish he'd stop hiding.

I'm still distracted when I get to my front door. As soon as I step inside I am met with the concerned eyes of my mother. They are red, like she has been crying. She reaches out and grabs my shoulders. She rarely touches me and my gut sinks.

"What's wrong, Mom?" My thoughts are all about Nan.

Mom sniffs as she runs her hands over my face. I am just about to tell her to get on with it when she lets out a sob.

"What happened to us, Talia?"

I freeze. What is she talking about? My face obviously reflects my inner confusion because she keeps going.

"To you and me. I love you so much. When did we fall apart?" She pulls me into a hug, and I feel like my brain will explode.

Were we ever together enough to be able to fall apart?

"Um, I love you, too." I pat her back and she squeezes me hard.

"You used to talk to me."

No I didn't.

"We used to do things together."

No we didn't.

I kick off my flats and guide my mom to the couch, where we sit.

"I don't know what you're talking about, Mom." I really have no idea what she is talking about.

"I miss you. You're always out. Sneaking around with that boy."

What? When did twice become always?

"That boy is no good for you by the way."

Don't I know it. I laugh and Mom's eyebrows sink. Her disappointment makes me angry. I want to yell, *I've been here the whole time! I never go anywhere and now that I have a life you suddenly want to be in it?*

But what I say is, "Sorry mom. We'll do something soon, promise."

I pat her on the head, which is something I shouldn't have to do.

"I love you, Talia." She curls up on the couch, which is where she's been sleeping most nights my dad isn't home. This display of emotion isn't normal, and I want to ask her about it. She is always such an emotional fortress. I wonder if she's upset about Nan. I open my mouth to ask her but close it before any sound comes out. We never talk. It feels weird to be sitting with her like this so I stand.

"I love you, Mom. It'll be okay." I want to smile at her, but I can't so I just go to my room.

I might not be able to talk to my mom, but I do want to talk to *somebody*. I stare at Janna's phone number and the little button that says 'send message' on my phone. Habit.

I want to text Lachlan to tell him what just happened with Mom, but I can't do that either.

I start to dial Nan's number and throw my phone onto my bed. It's too late to phone her with how sick she is.

I flop down into the reading chair in the corner of my room and my arms and legs go limp. I slide down the chair until I look like a zombie, sprawled out staring at one spot on the wall.

I don't know how long I sit like that but judging by the crick in my neck when I stand up–a while. When did everything get so...complicated?

~

My hands shake violently as I hold a large pair of sewing scissors I brought from home.

"Nan, I can't," I say between sobs.

I'm standing behind her so I can't see her face but her back is rigid. She runs her hand over her braid one more time and tosses it over her shoulder.

"I can't either, Talia. I'm so sorry but I need you to be strong for me. Just this once sweet girl. Just this once."

Her voice is so quiet I can barely hear her. Or maybe it's because I'm crying so loud.

I grip the thick grey plait in my hand and open the scissors. Over her shoulder, I see Nan tightly clutch the hat I made her.

I close my eyes, and squeeze the scissors.

The sound slices through the last thread of composure I have.

The scissors fall with the hair, and the panic consumes me.

~

When I get home there's a card waiting for me on my bed. From Janna. About Nan.

Sorry, is all it says. I'm so sick of hearing the word sorry. What a stupid meaningless word.

I shove the card off my bed and fall onto the covers. I don't know how long it takes before I cry myself to sleep.

~

I still haven't recovered from cutting Nan's hair yesterday and I almost skip knitting club again, but my mom is driving me crazy with her total loss of emotional control. It wouldn't be so bad if Dad would just stay home once in a while. She's calmer when he's there.

"Talia!" Marybeth's voice slices through my thoughts.

"What?" The way I glare when I say it makes her jump back. Her eyes sparkle at the potential for drama but we're cut off by Georgina. She squeezes my knee. She knows. Lachlan must have told her.

"You're still taking my place at the shelter on Wednesday, right?" Georgina asks sweetly. "I know I said I would, but my old bones are extra creaky lately." She smiles that conniving smile. Volunteering with Lachlan. She needs to stop throwing us together in hopes we stick. I roll my eyes.

Marybeth scoffs. "She's been hanging out with that grandson of yours too long, Georgie. She's adopted his attitude."

Georgina's face sets into a neutral stare.

She doesn't look at anyone, but stands slowly, using the couch arm to brace herself. She puts away her knitting and leaves the shop. She doesn't move fast which makes it a lot more awkward to watch her knowing she's offended.

The jingle of the door makes me shoot out of Nan's chair and I sprint to the door, flinging it open. I practically run Georgina over just outside, forgetting she doesn't make good distance at her age.

I slow to her pace and reach for her hand. She's shaking, but I can't tell if it's nerves or she's upset. Her face betrays nothing. I am thinking of what to say, when her eyes suddenly glaze with tears.

"He's a good boy, Talia. He's such a good boy." She shakes her head lightly, and I squeeze her hand.

"He is, Georgina. He's a great guy." I'm not sure I believe it after what happened between us, but he's this woman's family.

"It's really not his fault my stupid child fell for that rotten man," she continues. I keep walking with her and nod. I'm not about to stop her from talking about the things Lachlan keeps locked away.

"From what I hear, rotten is a nice way to describe him."

Georgina wipes a tear from her cheek and

puts her arm around my waist, squeezing me. It's a very grandmotherly thing to do. If I didn't have Nan I would definitely take Georgina as my grandma.

"No child should ever see what he saw. No child should feel what he felt. I'm surprised he isn't worse." Her eyes lose focus and she shakes her head.

"Do you ever worry his dad will come back?" I think it's a legitimate question, but the way Georgina's looking at me I know I'm missing something.

"He didn't tell you?" Georgina shakes her head. I shiver in the cold October air as a shadow passes across me.

"Tell me what?" I ask.

Lachlan doesn't really tell me anything.

Someone clears their throat behind us and we both jump. I spin to face Lachlan, utter betrayal saturating his features.

"I haven't told her yet, Gram." His eyes dart from Georgina to me. "That I don't have to worry about my father anymore--because he's dead."

CHAPTER EIGHTEEN

Lachlan

If I could've spit fire with my words I would. With the amount of acid eating away at my stomach I wouldn't be surprised.

They both stand there, stupid fucking looks on their faces. Talia's huge scared eyes are not cute right now.

"You wanted to know so bad. There. You know. The poor troubled drug addict and his dead abusive daddy."

"Lachlan," Gram starts, but I throw out my arms in a way that says 'what are you gunna do about it now?'. I need to be somewhere else. For the first time in a long time, I want to get high. To numb out. Talia is making me feel things again, and I hate her for it. Gram and I were fine before her.

I spin and walk back to the car. I let out a frustrated growl and punch an electric box jutting up from the sidewalk. My knuckle splits on the metal but the pain is welcome. A distraction.

Suddenly I'm grabbed by the back of the shirt and dragged to a stop. I know it's Talia so I keep walking until she grabs my arm with both her hands and yanks.

"What!?" I step backwards. She needs to be out of my destruction path. I'm sure it'll be easy. Her tail will tuck and she'll scamper off like the scared sheltered girl she is.

She meets my glare with one of her own. She balls the front of my jacket in her fist with one hand and points a finger in my face with the other. The wind whips her hair across her face and leaves stir up around us. I have never seen this. Not from her.

"Listen, you jerk," she yells and pushes me hard. I fall back into the car and she steps in, closing the distance she put between us. She grabs me again and slams me back into the car.

"Seeing as violence is the only way you listen to anyone then I will make you listen." She grabs my face in her hand.

Whoa! I am not sure if I'm scared or turned on but this is a part of Talia I never thought existed.

I raise my hands, mostly so I don't grab her and slam her up against the car and kiss her in front of Gram.

"Georgina's protecting you! She was

defending you, and I was comforting her. Yeah, people think you are nothing but an ex-con druggie but what are *you* doing to prove them wrong, Lachlan?"

Okay, that one stings. I feel the all too familiar anger, but I'm too shocked by this burst of passion from Talia that I can't bring the anger to the surface.

That and she has a point.

"I–" I try and she cups her hand over my mouth.

"I swear, Lachlan McCreedy, if you say *sorry* one more time, I will never speak to you again."

She rips her hand away and stalks off. I'm dazed. But definitely turned on.

Talia glances over her shoulder. "I know how you see me, Lachlan. Like I'm weak and spineless, but at least I can admit it. I know I have problems, and I know what they are. But at least I'm not a coward. At least I can ask for help."

And just like that she's gone.

As if it's a message from the karma gods, and they hate me by the way, my phone buzzes in my pocket. I slump into the car as the burn of her words crawls across my skin. My scars all open up, my wounds gaping, waiting for the pain. I've felt a lot of pain in my life. I've been broken, had cigarettes put out on my skin, had sliced my own wrist open with a dull blade, but nothing hurt as much as the look on Talia's face when she called me a coward. I am a fucking coward.

Gram puts her hands on my face, and I lean forward so she can hug me. She runs her hand down my head until she cups my neck and puts her mouth to my ear.

"Isn't it lovely to know how much Talia cares for you?"

I lean back, completely confused. By the way she screamed at me, she definitely doesn't care for me. Gram sighs and pats my face like I'm a child who just doesn't quite get it.

"I think I'll drive today."

~

I get three texts before I actually head to Garrett's. They were pissed at how late I was last Sunday. I think they're getting tired of me. They don't even offer me drugs anymore. Violet is gone again, and Garrett looks like he's rotting from the inside out. All he says to me this time is, "I can't cover for you, dude."

I can't believe I used to be friends with these people. I can't believe I let them 'solve' my little problem.

But I still go. I still run for them. I'm running to the same place almost every time now. Deacon's.

I know it's Deacon who's dealing now, after I saw his little handoff at school on Monday. He had the nerve to do it right in front of Talia, but I blocked her. I said something stupid and she got mad at me, although I think she is *still* mad at me for the whole dead-dad-coward thing. Saying stupid things is the easiest way to make her walk the other way and pissing off girls is also something I excel at.

It's Tuesday, and it's late. I am on my motorbike. It's probably the last time I'll be able to ride it judging by the bite in the air. It's almost Halloween and decorations are scattered across lawns, lights strung around windows and cotton stretched along fences. I reach Deacon's place and park across the street.

It's also almost my birthday. I can't keep doing this running.

I fling the package over the fence and turn to leave.

"Well, ain't this some shit." Deacon strolls up the sidewalk.

My body freezes and the muscle in my jaw tightens. I hate this punk. No, it doesn't have anything to do with Talia, and the fact that this guy used to have his hands on her, kiss her, or I don't even want to think what else.

I walk past him, bumping his shoulder and

glaring down at him.

He flinches, and I swell with satisfaction. At least the little shit is still scared of me.

Once I am halfway across the street Deacon speaks again.

"See you around, *Lachlan.* Nice bumping into you." He emphasizes my name.

Slimy little fu–I take a deep breath.

"Oh, and just FYI... I see the way you look at her. Don't waste your time. She's too good for you, and it's only a matter of time before she figures it out."

If I go down, I'm taking you down with me, I think and smile. I reach over my head and give him the finger.

I'm glad he can't see my face, because I completely agree with him. Eventually she will figure it out.

~

So what do I do when I resolve that I need to leave Talia alone? How do I behave when I decide that Talia deserves much better than a screw up like me?

I show up at her house at midnight and send her multiple text messages that say **clack**.

Good job, shithead, I think.

I have to see her.

I'm just about to send another when she texts me back.

What is wrong with you? Do you know what time it is?

I smile.

I'm throwing stones. Go to your window.

A light flicks on in a second story window, and I'm glad her room is facing the street or this would have been awkward.

Her figure appears as she draws back the curtains. I text her.

I didn't know which window was yours ;)

CHAPTER NINETEEN
Talia

I'm glad Lachlan can't see me because I'm grinning like an idiot, and I shouldn't be. I'm mad at him but I'm starting to think I'll always be mad at him.

I sigh and let the curtain fall.

And that maybe I'm okay with that.

I lift my phone and text.

You are ridiculous. Who does that?

I steal one more look at him outside, leaning on his motorbike.

Oh boy, I'm in trouble.

Throwing on jeans, a pair of socks and a sweater, I pad my way down the stairs quietly. Mom is on the couch again, and I pause to watch her. She mutters in her sleep and turns to face the back of the couch. I suddenly get the urge to wake her up and tell her everything. I glance at the door then back at Mom. I'll talk to her soon. I have to. I wait until her breathing evens out then carefully open the door, grabbing my coat and shoes. I've never snuck out of the house before, and I'm shocked at how easy it is.

I run down the steps and out to the sidewalk. Lachlan hands me a helmet and smiles that crooked smile that I love to hate. Or hate to love? I don't know anymore.

I don't say anything, just put on my coat, shoes and the helmet and hop on behind him. Lachlan's wearing an old faded leather coat that feels stiff in the cold air.

He kicks the bike to life and we drive away. He takes hold of my arm wrapped around his waist and slides his hand down until his fingers touch mine. He laces our hands together and squeezes. It makes my stomach jump. I shouldn't feel this way about him. Or maybe I should. I'm so confused, but I know that it feels good to hold him.

The air snaps at my skin and cuts through my coat as we fly down the streets, but I feel warm, content and light when I'm on Lachlan's bike. The comfort of his body, the force of the wind and the sound of the motor soothes my nerves. Never would I have guessed that motorcycles would be one of the keys to calming my anxiety.

I laugh. My chest heaves and Lachlan shifts so he can see me. He has a questioning grin.

I laugh harder. I might be going crazy. I

can't stop. Eventually Lachlan has to pull over. We are on the bridge.

"What the hell, Hat Girl?" He turns his body to face me. I take off my helmet and wipe my face.

"I don't know," I hiccup. "I don't know what's so funny."

He steps off the bike and holds a hand out. I take it and hop off, putting my helmet on the seat. He walks me to the edge of the bridge, never letting go of my hand.

My breathing is slower, the laughing has stopped but I'm still grinning. I let go of Lachlan's hand to reach out for the metal railing. I press my stomach against it and watch the water rushing by. I wonder if the water feels the same way I do as is flows wildly to who knows where--completely lost and out of control.

Lachlan steps up behind me. I feel him even though he's not touching me. One hand on either side of me, he grips the metal railing of the long bridge that connects the two sides of our city.

The smile falls from my face and I spin slowly, until we're face to face. His dark features are scrunched up like he's in pain, or thinking hard about something. He leans forward, closing the tiny space we had between us. I think he's going to kiss me, so I close my eyes, knowing I shouldn't want his lips on mine the way I do.

His breath grazes my cheek and his lips brush lightly against the skin. Then he pulls back and I open my eyes.

That's it?

He sighs and presses his body closer to mine, making me tingle from head to toe.

"I'm a drug runner." His voice is tight and falters a little at the end.

It's like a slap in the face. The tingling turns cold, more out of shock than anything else.

"What?" I heard him but my brain isn't computing.

"The text messages, that house... Deacon's. I run drugs for a local dealer."

I open my mouth a few times. It seems like it's physically painful for him to say it. His eyes won't meet mine so I reach for his face and force him to look at me.

"Why?" I had so many questions, especially about Deacon but this is what I settle on.

"I owe them. From before."

"From before you went to Juvie?"

He nods as my hands slide down, and I clasp them behind his neck. I'm way less concerned about this than I should be. I should be running, screaming, angry, disappointed, anything but what I actually feel. Relief. I'm happy. Happy that he's talking about it. Glad that he felt he could tell me. Even if it did take me calling him a coward to pry it out of him.

His body is tense as it presses against me. I rub his arms trying to make him relax. He doesn't.

"Yeah." He's staring blankly over my head.

"Isn't that why you went to Juvie? For drugs?"

Lachlan smiles the saddest smile I've ever seen. It tears me in half. He tilts his head toward me.

"I guess." He's distant, unfocused, and I can almost see the little reel of memories playing behind his eyes.

"You guess?" I ask. Shouldn't he know why he went to Juvie?

"They helped me keep my mom safe. From him. I was stupid. I just wanted someone to care. About me." His voice is still soft and distant. My body has gone cold.

I don't have to worry about him anymore— because he's dead.

"Lachlan? You didn't?" My voice is shaking. He glances down at me and his eyes widen.

"Fuck no! No I didn't kill him. Mom didn't mean to. She pushed him off me. He was drunk and he fell. He tripped and hit his head. It was an accident."

I'm holding my breath. This can't be real. This doesn't happen to people. Not people I know. Not people I care about.

"But surely she wouldn't go to jail if she was just protecting you?"

"We tried to lie about it. She told me it was the only way. That the law didn't care about people like us. I guess she was right because we both ended up in jail. She said it was my fault. That I provoked him. My dad, he didn't care about anything. My mom only cared about him."

He focuses on me again. "Sorry, you probably don't want to hear this. It sounds so crazy out loud. Probably why I hate talking about it."

I pull his face is closer to mine.

"I want to hear whatever you want to tell me." Nan had said that to me once, and it made me feel better, like I could trust her. I hope Lachlan feels the same. I want him to trust me.

Lachlan relaxes into me, pinning me harder against the bridge railing. He presses his face into my hair, and I tilt my head to the side. I feel his warm breath on my neck then his lips. He kisses all the way up to my ear, then along my jawline. I'm glad the railing is behind me because I can't feel my knees.

He leans back, and our eyes lock.

"I should stay away from you, Talia."

"I know," I reply unable to look away from the lips I want on mine. "But I don't want you to."

Lachlan's hands release the railing and grab me around the waist. He presses his lips to mine and pulls my hips into him. It's more than I can take and a sound escapes me I've never heard before. Blood surges through me, my head, my ears, my heart...other places.

We move against each other, pressing our lips, tongues and bodies together tightly as if we were trying to become part of one another. After he explores my mouth he moves his lips to my chin then long the other side of my jaw and down my neck. His hands rake the entire length of me until he wraps his arms around my waist and lifts my feet off the ground. My legs go around him instinctively. He sits me on the railing of the bridge and I hold onto him entwining my fingers into his curls. My body vibrates with a lust for him so strong it makes stars pop behind my eyes as he presses harder against me.

I've never felt this way before. My head goes back as I enjoy the small explosions of intensity going off in my entire body. I'm

100% into whatever Lachlan wants right now and by the feel of it he is too.

He pulls away and sucks in a raspy breath.

"Do you have any idea what I want to do to you right now?" he says against my mouth.

I smile. I have a pretty good idea.

"I need to take you home before I try them right here."

~

Lachlan dropped me off at home an hour ago and I'm still wide awake, staring at the ceiling. I'm agitated. Frustrated. Vibrating. My mind plays over our kiss and every time a new wave of tension fills me to the point I feel like I'll combust. Part of me is glad that his Southern gentleman side came out and insisted we stop. No one wants to know what the other part of me feels.

My head and my heart are still at war about what to do with Lachlan. But I do know my body wants nothing but him.

I try to kick the tension out by shaking my legs.

That doesn't work so I pull the blanket up right over my head and my hands pick up where his left off.

CHAPTER TWENTY

Lachlan

Usually my body takes over. If tonight happened with any other girl I would be post sex right now. Probably sleeping, or trying to figure out how to get out of bed without the girl noticing.

Talia. Talia is so different. I feel something when I kiss her. Not just needing a release, but needing to be her release. I feel it everywhere. I feel passion, not escapism. I feel alive, not empty. That gaping hole where my heart should be feels filled in. Not just with her, but with me. How I feel when I kiss her is more than just her. I want to be better. I believe I can be better.

So much so, I actually do homework when I get home. How fucking lame is that? I have the hottest kiss of my life and it makes me want to do homework.

~

I tap my hands on the steering wheel

while I wait for Talia outside the hospital. She's there for her Nan's treatment, and even though it makes me uncomfortable, I offered to pick her up. We have to go to this thing for the craft show anyways.

She walks out of the front doors, that big multi-colored bag slung over her shoulder. Probably filled with hats. She's smiling, which I take as a good sign.

She gets in and leans across Gram's car to kiss me. I run my hand over her cheek. Her eyes are a little red but she looks okay.

"You okay?"

She smiles. "I'll be okay. It's just hard. The doctors have decided to keep her in the hospital until she's done her treatment. She's throwing up a lot and she lives alone so they just want to make sure she's okay."

"I want to make sure you're okay. Did you have an attack?"

"Just one."

I feel bad for her. She told me all about how her Nan and I are the only ones who can calm her. That the song Gram used to sing to me to make me feel better, does the same for her. I don't say anything. Not good in these situations. Instead I just try to put all the things I can't say into a kiss.

She pulls back and rummages through her bag, pulling out a bluish grey ball. She gives me the yarn and I frown at her.

"What's this?" I ask.

"Happy birthday. It's another hat." She blushes.

I reach over and hold out my hand. She places hers inside.

"I kinda like you, Hat Girl." I wink at her and she tilts her head down, her hair falling in front of her face. Her shy sheltered-ness is back to being cute. I still have that urge to corrupt her though--to get through that innocence. I feel guilty every time.

~

At the doors to the arena Talia lets go of my hand as she turns to me and frowns.

"I forgot to tell you," she says. "The director of the show is Deacon's grandmother."

My heart sinks. I hope Deacon hasn't said anything to her.

Why would he? He's just as guilty. Even though I know it's true, guys like him get away with a lot more than guys like me, and I can't help but feel judged before I even see her.

"Okay," I say.

Talia snorts.

"She's the world's most evil grandmother, Lachlan. You'll see. She's nothing like Nan, or your Gram."

Talia holds the door open but doesn't go through. I'm just about to ask her what's up when she turns back to me.

"Speaking of which, you still haven't told me about Deacon's involvement in... um, what you do."

I slide my arm around her waist and distract her by kissing her neck. I feel her weaken in my grip, and I have to admit I really like the effect I have on her. I brush her hair to the side really slowly with just my fingertips. She shivers and I smile while placing a kiss on her hairline just behind her ear.

"Baby, it's my birthday. I don't want to talk about that right now. Well talk about it. I promise."

She looks over her shoulder at me. I know I have to tell her. I will. Just not today.

"You've been saying that since–"

I capture her mouth with mine and her words are absorbed into the motion of our tongues.

"I promise. I'll tell you everything," I whisper against her lips. "It's just hard for me. My mouth is great for a lot of things. Talking not being one of them."

I kiss her hard again and she spins to face me. She pushes me away playfully.

"Not fair." She grabs a fistful of my jacket

pulling me in for one last quick kiss. "And don't call me baby." She smiles and disappears through the door.

I watch her walking away. I should be on a post kiss high with the girl I'm crazy about, but instead I'm filled with dread. I'm not stupid. I know she's letting me get away with not talking.

I just wonder for how long.

~

As soon as we enter the conference room, I know exactly what Talia means about Deacon's grandma. She's a tall, thick woman with grayish black hair. It's pulled back into a bun that tightens her face at the eyebrows. The air is thick with her superiority and I instantly don't like her or her three-piece business suit. Gram wore dusty rose sweaters with birds and glittery snowflakes on them and the ugliest pleated 'slacks', as she calls them. That's what Grams' should wear.

"Talia." Deacon's grandmother holds her hand out to Talia and shakes it. Her eyes barely skim over me before she's sitting down at the table.

So that's how it's gunna be? I gesture for Talia to sit in the chair and I lean against the wall behind her.

"So Talia." Even the woman's voice

irritates me. I don't like the way she says Talia's name.

"I've just heard that your hats have passed the jurying process, which means you can sell them at the show. I just want to remind you, however, we have a reputation here and do everything we can to uphold it."

I have to cover my mouth to keep from laughing so I pretend I'm scratching my chin. Who the hell does this woman think she is?

Talia's head hangs, her shoulders tense and her back heaves as her breathing speeds up. Deacon's grandma continues, completely oblivious to her effect on Talia.

"I've also talked to the director of the shelter and he informed me of an incident of inappropriate behavior while volunteering."

Talia's hyperventilating now so I move forward to place a hand on her back, to show her I'm there. She jumps slightly. Super bitch doesn't even notice.

"So if you want to--cavort in basements, please do it on someone else's time."

Cavort?

"Do you understand, Talia?"

Talia isn't listening. She isn't focusing, and I know she's in the midst of an attack. I drop to my knees and spin her to face me. Gripping her face in my hands I start to hum softly. Her eyes dart frantically and short bursts of air come out her nose. I feel Deacon's Grandma watching me, and I should be embarrassed. But I only see Talia.

Suddenly her eyes find mine. I'm still humming, and I've moved forward so I'm between her legs. Her hands come up to my face as she recognizes me. She lets out one last long breath, which I assume means she is over the worst of it. I stand pulling her up with me and wrapping my arm around her protectively.

"Talia?" Bitch-lady says and I glare down at her.

"We hear you loud and clear, lady. Don't worry. I won't try and fuck her in basements anymore."

The look of horror on the woman's face makes my wholly unnecessary comment worth it. I didn't need to say it, but she already thinks I'm useless so why not use that to my advantage. I don't wait for her to reply either. I usher Talia outside. There are tears in her eyes but they don't spill out. I've never met someone who cries as much as Talia.

I'm proud of her for making it to the car.

"Why are you letting her bother you?" I'm irritated by how much it matters to Talia how people see her. I wish I knew how to make her see she's better than people like that. Better than people like me.

Fresh tears spill from Talia's eyes.

"It's not that," she says. "It's that I want to do this right. Nan always does it perfect. I'm just screwing everything up."

"Seriously?" is all I can muster. I reach into the back seat and grab the box of files that always stays in the car now. I open it up and papers are spilling out. I wave it in front of her face.

"What's this for?" She wipes tears with a gloved hand.

"This is your imperfectness."

She cocks her head to one side, confused.

I shake the box.

"This is everything you've screwed up." I start pulling papers out of the box.

"Here's the registration you didn't forget to file, and the volunteer logs that are immaculately filled out. The phone tree thing or whatever the fuck it's called that you drew up, with an actual tree on it." I'm flinging papers at her and she scrambles to catch them.

"Here's the booth plans you didn't forget to make or the decoration list that you've been harassing everyone about, which is annoying by the way."

She's smiling now, her fist is balled up as she chews her knuckles. I can't help but

ALLIE BRENNAN

laugh at her.

"It's not annoying," she says and I raise an eyebrow. "Okay fine, It's annoying."

"Your Nan is proud of you, Talia. You aren't her. You are you."

"Thanks, Captain Obvious," Talia says dryly, and I reach across the car and drag her over the console so she's sitting sideways on my lap.

She shrieks as we wrestle until she's laughing and glaring and threatening to pee on me. I've never been this guy.

"Okay okay, truce!" I say and pry her arm from around my neck.

Talia leans forward and rests her forehead on mine. She giggles again.

"What?" I ask.

"Did you see Greta's face when you said that thing about having sex with me in basements?" She giggles again and I smile.

"I thought she was gunna explode. I don't think I'll be welcome back to any planning events."

"No, probably not."

She kisses me quick before sliding back over to the passenger seat and my heart jumps a little. *God, I don't want to screw this up.*

"So." I slap my hands on the steering wheel. "Enough of the always-so-serious. It's

Halloween tomorrow, and we're going to go to a party."

Talia's lip twitches and her eyes narrow.

"I've heard that before. Before you took me to an addictions support group. Another thing that you refuse to talk about," she says lightly. It sounds forced.

I laugh. "No like a real party. A high school party. They're lame but we should go."

"Together? A high school party?"

I poke her arm. "You embarrassed of your ex-con boyfriend."

I slam my mouth shut. Talia's falls open.

"My what?"

For the first time in, I don't know how long, I am completely and utterly stripped of ego. I've never been a boyfriend. I've never wanted to be a boyfriend. I've never stuck around long enough to even skirt the borders of boyfriend-land.

I gulp. I'm nervous. Sweaty palms, shaking, afraid my voice will squeak, nervous. I've never thought about it until right this second, but what if she doesn't want me as a boyfriend? What if I'm just some secret fling? The bad guy she fools around with in high school before she settles down and does the right thing?

"Are you officially asking me out?" Talia has the biggest and most beautiful smile I've seen yet.

"Depends. Are you officially saying yes?" I try to sound like this whole thing was planned.

She flings herself back across the car and presses her lips to mine. Climbing over the console again she straddles me and I'm glad for the massive space in the Granny wagon. I let my hands slide up her and try to keep up with the way she's moving against me.

I break away for air and grin at her.

"So... That's a yes?"

"That's a yes."

I lean back and take in her expression. I never understood the boyfriend/girlfriend thing, but I'm starting to. Kind of.

CHAPTER TWENTY ONE

Talia

I'm standing in front of my mirror staring at myself worried that I'm not skinny enough or pretty enough or exciting enough. I have never stared at myself like this, not when I dated Jeremy in seventh grade, or Thompson in ninth grade, or even Deacon last summer.

I scrutinize my outfit, which is only half dress up because I don't really do dress up. I look stupid.

~

"Oh, darling, you look wonderful!" Nan says, but I can tell it takes her a lot of effort. She's wearing the white hat that was juried and has the hospital blanket pulled up to her chin. I don't like visiting her here. It doesn't feel right.

"Nan, I'm a burglar." I gesture down at my black leggings and tight black long-sleeved shirt. There's really nothing to it.

"No, no. I mean you. When did you get

such a nice bum?" she smiles and I feel my skin burn from my toes to the top of my head.

"Nan!" I yell. She doesn't know I brought Lachlan to meet her, and I hear him laugh in the hallway.

Nan glances at the door and Lachlan steps in. She smiles an apology to me.

"This is Lachlan."

He has his hands in his pockets, leaning his weight on one foot, hiding behind his super-cool persona.

Nan holds her hand out to him and his façade falters only for a second before he reaches out to her.

"I know who you are. Your grandmother and I have been friends for many years."

She pats his hand weakly. My heart breaks a little. I finally meet a guy I want Nan to know and she might not be around much longer.

Don't say that. She might beat it.

Lachlan waits at the door while I say good-bye. Nan kisses me on the forehead.

"I'm so proud of you, darling. I love you."

"Forever and always," I say.

~

I pull at the sleeves of my shirt as we drive to the party. It's too tight. I should have just worn something else. I adjust my black wool hat, and then tap my fingers on my leg.

Lachlan reaches over and takes my hand. I haven't been to a party since Deacon, because Deacon actually has friends. I don't. Now that I think about it, neither does Lachlan, well, other than his drug friends. My stomach ties in knots at the thought and I jump when he lets go of my hand and opens the door.

I can hear the bass pumping from outside, which causes my heart to speed up, as if it's trying to keep beat. Lachlan hooks his finger under my chin and pulls my face toward him.

"It's just a party, Tal. Just a party."

He's never called me Tal before and surprisingly it calms me right down. Janna always calls me Tal. *Called.*

He's right. It's just a stupid high school party.

Lachlan takes my hand and walks into the house like he lives there, pulling me in behind him. We fight through an ocean of shoes and thick hot air makes my forehead instantly sweat. Lachlan nods to some people hanging around in the hallway as we weave through. I am still amazed at how calm and collected he seems all the time. I feel like everyone is staring at me.

Wait. Everyone *is* staring at me.

Eyes follow me, some confused, some

shocked, some just mildly curious. I don't know if it's because I'm here with Lachlan or because I'm here at all.

"You look scared," Lachlan shouts over the music. "Just relax. Remember we're here to have fun."

He squeezes my hand and I do relax. Just a little. Then I see him. Deacon.

In the middle of the makeshift dance floor, Deacon and Janna are grinding against each other. It's disgusting and not just because he's my ex. They look wasted, sloppy. I don't remember Janna being like this. Ever. My first instinct is to rip her away from him and take her home. Then I remember we aren't friends anymore, and all the resolve to have fun is gone. I just want to be at home.

I turn to walk the other way. My arms are shaking and my legs feel weak. I make it only a couple steps before Lachlan pulls me into him. He wraps his arms around my shoulders and buries his head into my hair. He hums a few notes of our song and I count my breaths to slow everything down.

"Are you here with him, or are you here with me?" he says, his breath hot against my ear. A chill travels my spine and my arms go around him. He pulls back so he can find my lips with his and right there, in the middle of the party, he plants a kiss on me so deep my toes tingle. I'm dizzy when I pull back.

Okay now everyone is definitely staring. Lachlan guides me to the kitchen, and I stumble a little. As soon as we step onto the hardwood floor I hear a screech. Some girl I don't know is flying toward me, her arms outstretched. I try to step out of the way to let her pass but she follows me and slams her body into mine. She hugs me as she jumps up and down. I glance at Lachlan. I smell straight booze and my stomach turns.

Help me, I plead with my eyes. He does nothing, just laughs as I pry this drunk, I-don't-know-who, off me.

"Hat Girl!" she screeches again then turns around. "Becky, Amber! It's Hat Girl."

I'm so confused and people just keep bumping into me. I can't think straight in this gross, hot, noisy room.

How do people find this fun?

Two more girls come up to us. They're calmer and probably not quite as drunk.

These were the three girls in the hall when Lachlan asked me out the first time. They weren't 'the' girls but close. They look identical. Not in features, but the way their hair is straight, their lips are glossed, their jeans are tight and shirts too short. They even stand the same way.

"So when do we get our hats?" one of the

new comers asks. "We've been asking Lachlan, but he just won't give it up. He says he's not your agent."

The girl pouts at Lachlan and walks her fingers up his chest. I'm too confused to be at all jealous.

"Your hats?" I stutter and the screecher laughs, pointing at my head. Lachlan steps behind me and grabs my other hand so he has both, I lean back against him and watch the girls flick their eyes between our hands and each other. His arms wrap around me and he rests his chin on my shoulder.

"You'll get your hats soon, ladies. At that Christmas show at the arena. You can buy a hat and support the homeless."

Lachlan winks at them and then playfully nuzzles his nose into my neck. He's putting on a show and these girls are eating it up. I'm not sure why he's doing it, but he continues, "If you don't mind, I didn't come here to talk hats. I came to dance with my girl."

He spins around and I have to follow because his arms are still wrapped around my waist. I turn my head so I can see him, forgetting about those girls, and he kisses me.

"Let's dance. The music is terrible, so why not try for something good out of it?"

I scrunch my nose. "What can you possibly

get from this music that's good?"

I don't even finish when he spins me around pressing my body against his, his hands grabbing my hips.

Oh.

I get it.

I'm super awkward and uncomfortable on a good day, and now I'm swaying to music I hate, with a guy that makes me feel things I shouldn't, next to my ex-friend and my ex-boyfriend who look like they are full-out doing it with clothes on. Saying I feel uncomfortable is an understatement. I feel like a cardboard cut-out, stiff and plain. Bland and unexciting.

Deacon doesn't notice me. I have a feeling Janna doesn't even know where she is. The way she is draped over Deacon, her arm hanging limply at her side, her always perfect red curls tangled and covering her face, makes me sad. This isn't Janna.

Lachlan gets my attention by making fun of the song that's playing. He's dancing outrageously mimicking people in the music videos, that exaggerated sexy and dramatic movement. I'm half embarrassed because everyone is looking at us again, but I can't stop laughing. This is a side of him I didn't think existed. Brooding, moody, and mysterious–yes. Goofy, fun-loving and hilarious–not so much. I still feel it's a show. Happy is not a go-to emotion for either of us.

Lachlan puts his hands on my hips and moves me so I sway erratically like him. I try to pull his hands away but he holds on tighter. I shriek as his fingers tickle me and fight harder. The tempo of the music makes me break a sweat. The three girls, I can't remember their names, have joined us. We're all dancing and laughing.

This is fun. I'm having fun.

Something hard slams into my back and I fall into Lachlan. Whatever hit me falls to the floor, and I spin to see what happened.

Janna is lying on the floor. Her body is convulsing. Her hair is plastered to her face and her skirt has ridden up too far. I stare at her. My heart stops. My eyes dart up to meet Deacon's wide stare but his gaze flickers to Lachlan. They exchange a glance, but I don't have time to decipher it because a choking noise sounds above the music. Janna throws up. I drop to my knees and heave her onto her side. The puke spills from her mouth and blood starts oozing from her nose. I glare up at Deacon again. His eyes are still wide but distant. I don't think he knows what's going on.

"Help me!" I yell. Deacon just stands there so I find a beer bottle on the floor and throw it at him. It hits him in the shin and he focuses on me.

"Deacon, what's she on?" I ask. Someone has cut the music. Deacon doesn't answer.

"What is she on?" I scream at him, but it's Lachlan that answers me.

"Cocaine."

I shift my eyes frantically toward Lachlan when Deacon runs from the room. Lachlan's face goes dark. Shadowed. Angry.

He steps toward the door, and I grab his pant leg. He yanks the material from my hands without slowing down. There's an ominous hunch to his shoulders. A vision of him punching the metal electric box on the street flashes through my mind.

This is not good.

I can't leave Janna.

"Someone call an ambulance." I scan the room and about 5 people lift their cell phones. A few people say they already have.

I grab the person closest to me and pull them to the ground. Janna's shaking so hard that I can't hold her down with one arm.

I'm trying to be focused, but everything is blurry. I don't know who I'm looking at, but I grab their shirt.

"Keep her on her side. Don't let her roll over. Don't let her flail."

I don't wait for an answer. I shoot up and

sprint to the door, clearing the pile of shoes in one jump.

The cold air slams into me, but I don't stop. I'm running down the driveway. I have no idea where I'm going, I just go. I spot them just behind a big SUV.

Deacon's on the ground and Lachlan is on top of him. They're both bleeding, but Lachlan keeps hitting him.

I scream at them to stop. The shaking starts. In the distance I hear sirens. My breath is sharp and fast. I scream again just as I reach them. My vision is starting to blur. I grab Lachlan's arm, but he's too strong for me. He doesn't even know I'm here. I have to let go before he drags me right into the middle. *What do I do? Nothing if you panic.* I put my hand on my chest. I have to calm down. I can't panic. Not now. I have to stop Lachlan before he seriously hurts Deacon.

"Get out of the way," someone yells, and I step to the side.

Someone tackles Lachlan and knocks him off Deacon. Deacon scrambles backwards, and I go for Lachlan. He's yelling at the guy holding him down. The words coming from his mouth are horrifying and unrepeatable. He thrashes on the ground until he throws the guy off.

Lachlan goes for Deacon again, and three

more guys are on him. I'm sinking deeper with every punch, every curse, every step. I'm drowning in his anger as if it were my own. My vision blurs and sounds become muffled as I fill with tears. My heart breaks for him because I know it's his method. I know he can't turn it off just like me and my panic attacks. My heart also breaks for me, because I can't be with someone like this. I can't handle someone like him. It's too much. I am too screwed up on my own to deal with this. I had told Lachlan before that at least I knew I was emotional–that I had problems, but I never thought about my limits. I'd never thought what I would do if he was too much to handle.

Please keep this in mind when Lachlan is being...difficult. The words of his addictions councilor bounce through my head. This is what she meant. It has to be.

I wrap my arms around my waist and continue to take in Lachlan being *difficult.* I know he cares for me, but I can't do this–no matter how I feel when he is close.

Lachlan doesn't stop. He doesn't stop when the cops show up. I'm still sinking into the pavement. I can't move as the cop elbows Lachlan in the face and he goes down. I can't breathe as two cops kneel on Lachlan's back while a third cuffs him. I can't watch when they drag him painfully to the car and toss him, kicking and swearing inside.

"Talia!" Lachlan's voice pierces the air. Through streaming tears his figure is blurry but I can tell he's still struggling against the cops.

"Talia, I'm sorry. I should've told you."

I raise my hand to my mouth to stifle a sob.

"I should've told you everything. I'm so sorry."

The cops finally got him in the car and slam the door, but he's still yelling.

My feet are rooted and my head shakes back and forth as sobs wrack my body. I have no idea how I'm still on my feet. I have no idea why the panic hasn't consumed me.

Deacon is standing next to me. There are lights flashing everywhere. The ambulance sirens are going off as they haul Janna to the hospital. We stand and watch silently.

Deacon wipes blood from his face and looks over at me, but I don't meet his gaze.

"Stay away from him, Tali." He smiles. This is not the time to smile.

"He's a drug peddling asshole. Don't think he won't hit you next."

Says the guy who just ran away from his overdosing girlfriend. He probably gave her the drugs too. Slowly I turn to him.

I slap the smile right off his face. "Fuck you, Deacon."

CHAPTER TWENTY TWO

Lachlan

White hot heat rips through my hand and I double over in my seat. The cop won't take the cuffs off until the Doctor sees me.

I'm a flight risk apparently.

I breathe through my teeth until the searing pain becomes a dull throb. It's definitely broken. One more deep breath to inhale more of the disgusting sanitized death smell and I lean back. I hate hospitals. I wonder how Talia could stand spending so much time here.

"You okay, kid," the cop asks. I glare at him. My forehead wrinkling making the dried blood pull at my skin.

"Lachlan McCreedy," the nurse yells from the front. I stand and a wave of nausea passes through me from the pain. The cop grabs my upper arm, and I'm glad because I feel like I'm going to pass out.

I clutch my wristband in my good hand,

and rub the leather with my thumb. I had to take it off because of the swelling.

I'm only half paying attention as the cop leads me through the big glass sliding doors.

She's standing on the other side. There is blood on her face, just along her jaw line and I feel like I've succeeded. It's a horrifying, stomach clenching feeling.

The sheltered innocence is gone. Her features are hard, her blue eyes no longer the color of ocean waves but stormy black. I've succeeded in dragging her into my world.

Her eyes never leave mine as the cop walks me down the hall to x-ray. I watch her until my head is turned as far as it will go. The cop shakes my arm and I grit my teeth, clutching the wristband even tighter.

Forgiveness.

I open my fingers and the band falls silently to the floor. I see her one more time as I'm hauled around the corner. She's staring at the band. Tears sliding down her cheeks.

I did this to her. With everything that has happened to me, everything I've done, *this* is the moment. The moment I truly want forgiveness. I just waited until it was too late.

CHAPTER TWENTY THREE
Talia

I had to know if he was okay. If Janna was okay even though I knew they'd never let me see her because I'm not family. Now that I've turned Lachlan's wristband over in my hands a thousand times, I wonder if I'm okay.

My head falls back against the soft headrest of Georgina's car. I'm glad Lachlan left the keys in it but it smells like him and it's bothering me. My head falls to the side and I try to imagine what's going on in there. By the swelling of his wrist, I'm sure Lachlan broke something. Part of me hopes it hurts as much as I do.

I've never known anyone who did drugs so I can't imagine Janna, and what they are doing to help her. Pumping her stomach? But cocaine is snorted so it couldn't be in her stomach? I have no idea.

I sigh. Lachlan's right. I do live under a rock. Right now I want to crawl back under it and never come out.

~

My dad's home when I get back from the hospital. He's not supposed to be home until next week.

His black four-door is in the driveway. His shoes are at the front door beside a suitcase. My heart jumps. Why is there a suitcase beside his shoes?

I can't handle one more thing. Not tonight.

Slowly I peek around the wall that divides the entrance from the living room. My parents are sitting on the couch, looking at each other. My mom's eyes are red and swollen. She's cross-legged in those ridiculously expensive sweat pants that make you look like you work out. Her light hair is pulled off her face into a ponytail. I don't remember the last time she wore a ponytail. My heart is thundering so loud I am sure they can hear me.

Is he leaving? Is my dad leaving?

My mom notices me and she sits up straighter.

"Talia, honey, come in here for a sec." She smiles and holds her hand out to me.

Something feels weird. My dad is straight-faced and pale. He nods to me to sit between them. I haven't sat between them like this since they told me Pops had died when I was six. I barely remember what it's like.

I sit and lean back into the couch cushion so I can see both of them. I'm shaking with nerves. *Just say it already,* I want to scream.

"Talia," my father says, with his deep voice which means it's serious. "Talia, your mother and I have something to tell you." He pauses and turns to Mom. Is he blushing? He fidgets in his seat and nods to her.

"You're breaking up, aren't you?" I try to stand. Mom grabs me and yanks me back down.

"Don't be ridiculous, honey. Your father and I are *not* getting a divorce. Breaking up! Good lord, we're not in high school."

She laughs, and now I am totally confused.

"Then what's with the oozing solemn vibe?" I ask. "And why is dad blushing?"

This makes dad blush even more and he clears his throat.

"Your father and I have been having some troubles, yes. But darling, when you love someone you just make it work. Sometime the fire dims but it doesn't go out. Not if you don't let it."

Mom glances at dad and he smiles in agreement.

"But that's not what we need to talk about." She waves her hand.

"Trouble?" I wasn't sure if I wanted to

know with all this talk of flames. I am an only child and I'm convinced I was conceived on the honeymoon and they've never seen each other naked since.

I must be wrinkling my nose because mom pushes it with her finger. She laughs again. It's a different laugh than usual, a real one.

"You used to make that face when I fed you anything with cabbage in it."

My dad laughs too and squeezes my knee. "She still does."

They lock eyes and I am suddenly super uncomfortable. I've intruded into a private space that is just theirs, but I can't help but watch them. They really do love each other. It's obvious now that I look at them, like, *really* look at them.

"So, you guys are okay then?" I drag the words out. I'm still confused about the suitcase and the 'talk'. "We're still okay?"

"We will be, honey," Mom says and pats my leg.

Will be means they aren't right now? Dad must have sensed my confusion because he pulls me into him and kisses the top of my head.

"Life gets in the way sometimes, sweetie. We were so busy providing for our family that we forgot to actually be one."

I lean against my dad's chest. It's been a

long time. I realize how much I missed him.

"I miss you," I blurt. I don't mean to say it out loud. My dad squeezes me tighter.

"I'm so sorry, sweetie."

I lean back. No more sorrys. No more crying over my problems and expecting them to go away.

"You're never here. You're never around. How are we supposed to be a family when we all just do our own thing?"

"I know darling," Mom says. "That's what we're going to work on."

"How? Dad is always gone because of his job. I liked the way it was before better. When he worked here. Not for some stupid corporation. So what if he makes more money?"

"I'm working on that." Dad squeezes my shoulder.

"But first we have to fix ourselves," Mom says. "We're going to have to because our trio is no longer."

I can't look at her fast enough. "What?"

She can't be.

"I'm pregnant, sweetie. You're going to have a baby brother."

My eyes would fall out of my head if I opened them any wider. This has to be the most bizarre and emotionally draining weekend of my life.

"But, how, when... I..." I stutter and my dad squeezes me again.

"We're not as old as you think we are," he says and chuckles. I think about my parents having sex. It's gross. I mean obviously I get it, but I can't help but be grossed out. They're my *parents*.

"When?" I finally ask.

"June." Mom rubs her belly. Suddenly it makes sense. Her being so emotional. Crying all the time. Confronting me about how we aren't the perfect Mother/Daughter team at the debutant ball.

"Um, congratulations," I say awkwardly. "So what's with the suitcase then?"

"Your father and I need a little alone time. To figure this out. It's just as surprising for us. We're heading out for a week to a little B&B just outside of town. It's going to be so romantic. There is a sauna and hot tub and private Jacuzzi."

"Stop, Mom." I cover my ears. "Seriously."

They are both laughing at me, and I manage to smile.

"Fine, lips sealed," Mom says. "And you're almost seventeen now so we trust we can leave you alone for a whole week, and you won't get into any trouble with that trouble-maker boyfriend of yours." She smiles like she joking, but her eyes say she's serious. I drop my gaze to my lap, my own smile fading.

"Lachlan and I aren't together. So no need to worry about trouble. I'll probably just have a TV marathon and knit. I have a million hats to knit in a month."

Mom grabs my shoulders and pulls me to her so hard it knocks the wind out of me.

"Oh, sweetie, honey. I'm sorry to hear that. Are you okay?" She's stroking my hair and face and shoulders. My face is squished against hers so tight I couldn't talk if I wanted to.

Is it going to be like this until June?

I'm not sure when my life became so complicated.

"I'm fine, Mom. When do you leave?" I try to change the subject and pry myself out of her grip.

"Tomorrow morning," Dad says.

I know that a baby in the house will affect me big time. But maybe this is what we need to bring us back together? I also know that I'm exhausted, which is a good thing. If I have to think for one more second my brain is going to revolt completely and refuse to ever function again.

~

It snows for the first time on Monday. Like, really snows. By noon there's a thick layer of the cold sticky flakes blanketing the ground. I run outside between classes, to my parent's car, to grab my dreaded math book. By the time I come back in there are snowflakes stuck in my hair and eyelashes. There's a blast of hot air when I open the school door and my nose is filled with radiator dust and a slight wet dog smell. It makes me wish for the wool shop. Or the smell of Lachlan, spice and laundry.

I turn the corner and lose all the warmth the entrance heater provided. Deacon's leaning against my locker. His jeans are perfectly straight and pressed. His button up plaid shirt ironed and un-tucked. His sandy hair hangs in his eyes like he purposely does it that way. He looks like Deacon, perfectly put together. Everything but his face. Lachlan left his mark.

Deacon's eye is bruised green and black, his lip scabbed.

I stop a couple feet from him, and he lifts his head.

"You okay?" he asks.

I frown.

"I'm fine. Why?"

He smiles his winning smile and I want to slap him again. He knows something.

I step up to my locker and ignore him but he doesn't leave.

"Lachlan isn't here today."

My frown deepens into a glare.

"What's your point, Deacon?"

"Cops called me last night. Said they want me to come in and make a statement. I thought they'd have called you, too."

My heart starts hammering.

"No, they haven't," I say, trying to keep my voice even.

"That guy's no good, Talia, and you know it. I'm sure it was fun to slum for a while, but seriously."

A gagging sound crossed with a scoff comes out of mouth. I can't speak because my chest has started expanding and contracting too fast. Deacon no longer matters. I think of Lachlan, and clutch his band that I now wear on my own wrist. I try to hum our song in my head and it works. I throw off the blanket of panic. Alone. By myself.

Leaning back onto the lockers, I savor the moment.

I can see Deacon gawking, I know what he just told me is big. That Lachlan is in a lot of trouble. But just for two seconds I want to revel in my success. I beat it.

I over came it.

All alone.

I laugh and hug my text book tighter to my

chest.
    Beautiful irony.

CHAPTER TWENTY FOUR

Lachlan

I shift my weight trying to get into a position that doesn't hurt my arm. I lay on my back resting my hand on my stomach. I'm still not comfortable, but I don't think the discomfort is on the outside. I can handle physical pain. What I can't deal with is this gnawing guilt that I really screwed it all up. I knew I would, but this time I wanted it to be different. This time I wanted to do the right thing. Problem is I can never make a decision until it's too late. I want to tell her everything, when she's no longer willing to hear it.

The TV isn't working to distract me so I stare out the window and take slow breaths, inhaling whatever amazing thing Gram is baking. I won't get any. Gram hasn't spoken a word to me since she picked me up at the hospital yesterday, and this wouldn't be the first time I won't be *allowed* dessert. I swear she's deliberately baking just to deny me.

When I asked to skip school today she only pursed her lips and gave a short nod. Probably to have me around all day to rub my nose in what a disappointment I am. Not that I blame her.

My phone buzzes and my heart stops. I glance over at Gram who glares and turns her back.

How could I ever prove myself to Talia if I am nothing but a disappointment to my own family?

I dig the phone out and look at it.

Deacon said the cops called him. Just thought you should know.

I feel like a bag of bricks dropped on my chest. Not because of Deacon, or the cops. Because she didn't ask how I was. I'm like a fucking little girl around her. She shouldn't be concerned about me. She shouldn't have texted me at all.

I set my phone down and pick it up a dozen times before text back. I want to say sorry. To ask her to forgive me. To hide behind the fact that I have a past. I can't anymore.

She always chose him. She did everything he said, no matter who it hurt. She lost herself in him and I paid the price. But you. You don't put up with any of it.

With everything you go through. You're amazing. Just thought you should know.

I barely put the phone down when it buzzes again. I scoop it up, hoping it's from Talia.

408 10ᵗʰ Ave

A surge of, what I think is bravery, jolts through my body. I text back *I'm done. Get someone else.*

I hit send and immediately regret it.

Not bravery. Stupidity.

I get a text almost immediately.

You're done when we say you're done...

CHAPTER TWENTY FIVE
Talia

I'm unable to stop staring at my phone, but also unable to form any response to Lachlan's text. I toss my phone on the dresser and go downstairs. The house is empty. My parents left this morning, leaving the keys to Mom's car on the island. I glance at the keys then turn to the entryway.

I should be happy that I get to be truly alone. No parents. But the house feels bigger, colder and less lived in with them gone.

I swipe the keys off the counter and leave the house.

~

Nan's sleeping when I get to her hospital room. She looks worse every time I see her. She's losing so much weight. Her eyebrows and eyelashes are gone, and she keeps getting these bruises on her arms and legs from the most minor bumps.

I stand in her doorway, wondering

whether I should go in. But I didn't bring my knitting bag so I really have nothing to do.

Maybe Janna is still here. My stomach turns. I should go see her. I don't really want to but I should.

She's awake when I get there. There are no tubes sticking out of her like there is with Nan. She appears to be normal Janna, maybe a bit pale.

She smiles and gestures with her hand for me to come in. There's a lot going through my mind, most of it at war within my head. I want to hug her, slap her, scream at her and tell her it will be fine. I'm angry with her but so glad she's okay. She must sense it because her smile reaches her eyes and she gives a little nod.

I hold out my hand and she takes it. Her skin is warm and smooth, not clammy and cold like when I was holding her down at the party.

"How are you?" she says. Her voice betrays her lack of confidence and it wobbles. She still isn't sure which reaction I'm going to have.

"I'm fine, J. How are you?"

Like a light switched off her eyes go dark and fill to the brim with tears.

"I didn't mean to, Talia. Everyone is saying such awful things. Calling me the worst names. It's the first time I've done it, I swear."

The tears slide down her lightly freckled cheeks and she turns her head away from me then lowers herself so she's laying on her bed. I immediately move to sit next to her. I stroke her hair like Nan does when I'm upset.

"Who cares what people say. They don't matter."

Who am I to give advice? I care every single second of my life what other people think. Why else would I make sure they stayed as far away as possible?

Janna cries harder, curling into a ball and putting her head on my lap. She wraps her arms around my waist and we sit. Janna cries and I just sit, twirling her hair in my fingers like we used to do when we watched movies. She had the thickest hair I'd ever seen.

Finally she stops crying. I feel good that I can be there for her, but my stomach is twisting because I shouldn't be. I should be furious with her. I *am* furious with her.

"Why are you doing this?" She sniffs.

"Doing what?"

"Being so nice to me."

I've always been nice to her. She's the one who hooked up with my boyfriend.

"J, I watched you convulse on the floor in a pool of your own blood and foam at the mouth. I would never wish that on anyone, even after what you did."

Janna's face goes white and she buries her head in my lap again.

"I'm so sorry. So so so sorry! I–"

I shush her, not so much because I want to tell her it's okay, but because I want to tell her it's not okay. I want to say, you just can't do that. Make out with people's boyfriends. Betray your friends like that. Abandon people when they need you the most.

I think of Lachlan. I think of him in cuffs being dragged down the street and how he looked so out of place. He shouldn't. He's been to jail before. He's covered in tattoos and scars that symbolize the root of all the bad decisions he's made.

I'm starting to think maybe I abandoned him too. I've memorized the text message. I've played the night of the party in my head a million times for a million different reasons. I remember the way his eyes pleaded with me when he dropped the wristband. I should at least hear him out.

But I need time. The way I feel when he's close, I just can't risk being around him.

Janna shakes my leg.

"Talia? Where'd you go?"

I blink at her.

"I should go." I lift her head from my lap

and hop off the bed. Janna looks bewildered and slightly hurt.

"I'm sorry, I just. I'm just really confused right now."

"I know things are weird between us, but you can always talk to me. I miss you, Tal."

My head swims. The pressure of everything that's happened in the last few months presses against my mind. I want to tell her everything. I want to ask her why.

"I miss you too, J. I know I can talk to you. I just don't know if I'm, I'm–"

"Ready?"

I nod.

"Deacon is not a good person, Talia. I'm not making excuses for myself but when you're ready, I need to tell you what really happened. I need to tell someone, and you're the best friend I've ever had."

I pause at the door. "What do you mean, what really happened?"

Her eye's fill with tears again.

"I want you to know that I said no. To the kiss, I mean. I thought we were just friends. I was stupid, Talia. I understand if you don't believe me, but it's true."

A flash of that first day of school floods my mind.

Janna pushed him away, sliding down the rough wall. Her eyes were wide and scared as tears flowed. Her hand covering her mouth. She wouldn't look at me.

I move back to her bed and pull her into a hug. How could I not have seen that?

"I believe you, J. Of course I believe you." I hug her tighter and she sobs into my chest. Her whole body shakes.

"He told me it was my fault. That I led him on. That I was asking for it."

I start to shake almost as bad as Janna.

"It's not. Don't you dare think that." I'm overcome with the thought that I was once there. I remember how he held me and kissed me as I was trying to push him away. Deacon was used to getting his way. With me, my panic attacks always got in his way. He was afraid of them. He never went further because he was scared of me.

The tune starts playing in my head. Lachlan's total opposite reaction to me. His voice and how he just rocked with me and sang and held me until it was over.

I look down at Janna. I'm so torn between feelings. I've spent so long being mad at her, but it turns out I just wasn't there for her either. I didn't listen the day in the bathroom. I just assumed. She said he made her keep it a secret. Janna's so strong. I never thought anyone could force her to do anything... My stomach contracts.

"The party? What happened at the party? Did he?" I want to throw up.

Janna shakes her head. "No, my mom made them check me out once I was stable."

I close my eyes briefly and see Deacon's hands on her at the party. I knew that wasn't Janna.

"But that's what he was going for? With the cocaine? Getting you high?"

Janna shrugs. "I don't know. Probably. But you can't say anything, Talia. You can't. I don't know what I want to do yet. Technically he didn't do anything but kiss me a couple times but he could do worse to someone else. I just don't know what to do yet."

She's crying again.

"I won't say anything." I pull her close.

"I'm scared. You don't know him like I do. I should never have set you up with him. I...I knew he was dealing. I knew he was pushy. What if he had done something to you? I can't even...I'm just glad this whole thing was me and not you."

I push her back abruptly and stare into her huge green eyes. I don't know what to say. I shake my head. I just shake my head harder and harder until she pulls me back into a hug.

Like Lachlan, Janna has had to deal with something that no one our age should ever have to deal with. That no one of any age should have to deal with. I feel guilty. Janna took this for me. She held it in to protect me. Lachlan opened up to me. He trusted me and let me into his broken world. And what did I do? Abandoned them to wallow in my own broken world.

I should have listened.

To both of them.

~

Visiting hours are almost over and I'm still sitting on Janna's bed. She's laughing. I've missed that laugh. All the times she dropped everything to cheer me up, to snap me out of my darkest thoughts. I try to do the same for her.

Problem is that she's funny. I'm not.

We've been silent for a few minutes and she's eyeing me up like she wants to say something.

"Out with it." My mouth twitches. I know exactly what she's going to say. It's probably been driving her crazy for months.

She tucks her knees up to her chin. "So, Lachlan McCreedy? What's up with *that*?" She pushes my shoulder playfully. "Are you guys dating or something?"

"Yes," I say and my cheeks burn. "No. I mean, we were. I don't know. I haven't talked to him since the party."

She's nodding, and there's light in her

eyes. Janna loves boy drama. It gets her into trouble. Obviously. A wave of guilt hits me. Trouble I should have been there for.

Like a floodgate opening, everything pours from my mouth. From the first time Lachlan walked into the wool shop, to the date at the support group, to the kiss, to THE kiss, to the party, everything. It feels so good to talk to someone about it.

"I think he loves you, Tali." She sounds serious and I laugh.

"Yeah right. We're as different as two people can be, J."

She frowns.

"Are you?"

That shuts me up.

Aren't we?

~

I pick Janna up for school on Friday. She was released from the hospital but stayed home. I tried to convince her to stay home today too. Who wants to come to school just on Friday?

We get to my locker first and my heart freezes, colder than the November air.

Deacon's there, with this big, stupid, confused but horrified expression on his face, which is still bruised under the eye and scabbed on his lip from his fight with Lachlan. He looks from me to Janna and back again. Janna turns up her nose and walks past him, shoving him into the locker with her shoulder.

Deacon rubs the back of his neck. "I guess I deserve that."

He tries to smile that smile that won me over in the first place. I feel like I'm going to puke.

Seriously?

"You deserve a lot more than being shoved into a locker."

"Fair enough, Tal. Listen I wanted to know if the cops called you?"

I slam my locker with a bit more force than necessary.

"No, why do you care so much?" I spit.

"Oh. I told them you were there." I don't think he expected me to talk to him like that. I have a feeling he hasn't clued in that Janna would have told me everything.

"So did you hear my Grandmother is trying to shut you down? Get you kicked out of the Charity Drive because of that Douche you've been dating?" he continues with a smirk.

Is he seriously smirking right now?

"What is this? Good news hour with Deacon Finnley?"

Deacon doesn't say anything, and I'm losing any patience, or curiosity, I had for him. My heart is vibrating, not beating, vibrating. There's an attack just at the edge of my mind. I can feel the thoughts starting to jumble. I force myself to take a deep breath and just stare. It's getting a tiny bit easier every time to keep them away, now that I'm trying.

"Is there a point, Deacon? Because I'm late for class."

He still just stands there. He's not used to me acting this way, but honestly neither am I. It's kind of exciting. This is Lachlan. Lachlan brought this out of me. I push the panic down and like Lachlan, I cross my arms coolly and put all my weight on my back leg. I raise my eyebrows as if daring Deacon to get to the point. He still isn't saying anything so I walk away.

Deacon grabs my upper arm as I pass him. I wince and try to yank my arm from his grip, but he won't let go. He glances behind me then narrows his gaze, staring down at me.

"I fixed it for you, Tal." He's trying to tower over me, to threaten me with his size. Lachlan has never used his size over me, and he's supposed to be the violent one. Even when he hauled Violet out of the support group it was like a mother ushering a misbehaving child from a grocery store. Deacon's squeezing and lifting. He pulls me close to him and looms over me with a look in his eye that's terrifying.

"I fixed it for you because I know about your Nan. I know this is important to her, so obviously important to you. I don't even get a thank you?"

I'm still jerking my arm, trying to get away. More frantically this time. How dare he use Nan against me.

I wish Lachlan were here. It hits me with so much force my whole body stops working. Realizing I'm falling for a guy while I'm being pushed around by my ex is a strange way to come to terms with the feelings I've been ignoring.

Deacon shakes me hard, and I feel the bruise starting to form but I fight harder. I set my face in defiance, like Lachlan would, and I stare him down with the same intensity.

"Fixed what?"

"The Charity thing. I convinced my Grandma to let it go, as long as he doesn't show up, you're good to go."

"Well aren't you a hero." My voice is like acid and his grip falters for a second before he tightens it so much I whimper in pain.

His expectant gaze makes me sink into a blinding fear. I'm trying not to think of what that look means. I feel it hang over my head. I feel the sudden weight of this 'favor' loom over me, shadowing me in Deacon's debt. He knows I'd do anything to make Nan happy. He knows this show is only important to me because of her. He's using Nan to get what he wants.

I'm flooded with thoughts of Lachlan, of what he owes people who have helped him. How he must have felt and how everyone just abandons him before they even get to know him. I want him. I don't want to abandon him because he's difficult. Because he's broken. We're both broken.

We're all a little broken.

We all harbor little pieces of pain that accumulate inside us. Pain we wish we could cast out, but in truth defines us. All we really need is someone to help us bear the hurt. Someone to say I'm right beside you. Someone to say no matter what you're not alone. I want that. I want to be that. For him.

I glare up at Deacon. Putting everything I have behind it. I choose who I owe. I choose who I want in my life.

"I don't owe you anything," I snap before he gets a chance to say anything. His eyebrows raise and he leans down so our noses are almost touching.

"Don't you?" He smirks, dropping my arm. There's definitely going to be a bruise. He's smirking. Why is he smirking?

"This works both ways, sweetheart. I can tell Grandmother to kick you out of your little artsy show *and* I can help send your boyfriend back to prison by slipping into my testimony how I saw him shaking you. Giving you that nice little bruise on your arm. I just asked him nicely to let you go. I didn't want it to escalate to a fight."

"You wouldn't. No one would believe you."

"Seriously, Talia? No one would believe that *he* would hit a woman? Isn't that why his mommy is in jail. Because his daddy beat the shit out of her and she finally killed him? I'd be careful how you talk to me. I know a lot more than you think I do. And plus if it came down to him or me... Who do you think they'd believe?"

My mouth won't work, and I watch him walk away rubbing the spot on my arm where his fingers were. He wouldn't. No one is that cruel.

A month ago I would have believed that. Right now, I'm not so sure.

Suddenly I'm hyper aware. I can feel someone behind me. I can smell the faint scent of spice and laundry. My thoughts are crystal clear as I realize Lachlan is standing behind me. Deacon knew he was there. He said all of that knowing that Lachlan was right there.

I spin slowly and expect to see that glazed fury in Lachlan's eyes. But I don't. His eyes exhibit pure pain. His face is tired, defeated.

"You are so much better than all this," he says.

I reach out to him, but he won't meet my eyes. My fingers brush the hard plaster of his cast as he walks by and pulls his hand away.

I lose him at the exact moment that I finally admit I've fallen for him.

CHAPTER TWENTY SIX

Lachlan

I see the wristband when she reaches for me. She is wearing it, and I feel a dizzying hope. Then I think of the way Deacon was holding on to her.

The hope doesn't last. I should know better than to think it would.

I'm crushed by the realization that I've succeeded in dragging her down. I'm involving her in the shit I'm trying to get out of. I can see the fear in her eyes. I see the recognition in her face of how far people will go to get what they want.

I don't give a shit about Deacon's threats. I'd gladly go to jail again if it protects her.

My phone buzzes.

Of course.

The rest of the day is a blur, and I don't have my first Talia-free thought until Gram and I are eating.

She taps her knobby finger on the table.

"I spoke with your mother today," she says. She's talking to me now in short spurts. I've never seen her so angry with me, and this really isn't the worst I've ever done. Maybe she's getting tired of me, too.

I look up. "Oh yeah?"

"Her parole hearing is in one month. They are moving it up. Good behavior or something like that."

"Really? For a murder charge? She's only been in for a couple years."

I always tried to take the brunt of his shit but he always found a way to get us both. Even in death.

"Well it's not for sure, son. And your father's death was accidental. It's not a murder charge. Manslaughter, and they went easy on her because of what your father did to her. You know that, so don't act like a child." Her mood swings were starting to disorient me. It was just a question.

My heart sinks and Gram reaches across the table to take my hand.

"It's just a hearing though," she continues. "They might deny her. We have to be prepared for that."

"I know, Gram." I squeeze her hand, but she doesn't let go.

I don't usually let these touches linger but ever since Talia, I have this growing urge to be close to someone. I almost want to climb into Grams lap like I did when I was a kid and cry. Almost.

"I love you, Lachlan. You know that right?" she's suddenly so serious it stops my breathing.

"I know, Gram." I squeeze her hand again.

~

It's Friday night, and I have to meet Garret tonight for what really is going to be my last run. It has to be. This has to stop. I shake as I walk through the snow to his front gate. I'm not nervous to tell him. I'm nervous that I made the wrong choice. I have a plan, and I've never had a plan before. I'm convinced it's going to blow up in my face, but I want to try. That's what scares me. That's why I shake.

Garret comes out to let me in, but I don't get a smile or a fist bump or a 'hey' or anything. He walks ahead of me and the sight of him makes me sick. How can he do this? Just be a bitch his whole life? Not have a single care other than getting high?

I stand and spread my arms and legs so Garrett can check me. He usually waits until after. But we're no longer cool so he checks me first before getting the dope.

"They're being watched," he mutters as he finishes checking me.

"What?"

"The dealer. He's being watched. I've been told we have to be extra careful now. Straight business." He runs up the stairs, and I watch the empty hall with my heart thundering. He comes down with a small duffel bag. That is a lot. Too much. If I get caught with that I'll be dead. Or I might as well be dead because I'll spend the prime of my life in maximum security.

"I can't take this, man."

"You can't?" He sneers and dumps the bag at my feet.

"No, I can't. I'm 18 now. If I get caught with this–"

"But you won't, Lannie. You know that. You're the best. You manage to be on Probation, go to drug counseling *and* run drugs without getting caught. No one's as good as you. That's why you have to do this one." He stabs my chest with his finger.

I'm speechless. How sad is it that my biggest talent is carting drugs from one fucking douchebag to another? Garrett stops in the doorway to his disgusting living room and looks over his shoulder at me.

"It's nothing personal. It's business. You know that right?"

I don't say anything. Of course it's personal. It's always been personal. This is punishment for telling them I was done. It's meant to scare me.

It's working.

I toss the duffel in the trunk because it's a bit obvious. I'm so tempted to look what's in it but I don't. The cardinal rule of running. Never look.

My phone buzzes and I am waiting to read Deacon's address but it's different.

1328 C King Street. Bay 4. Half an hour. Don't fuck with us on this one.

My heart starts to hammer in my chest and my breathing quickens. This must be what Talia feels like when she panics. It sucks. It really fucking sucks.

I throw Grams car in drive and make my way down the slippery streets. The closer I get the harder I shake. I can see the warehouse in the distance.

I don't want to. I don't want to do this anymore.

Stopping the car in the big parking lot, I hit the steering wheel with my good hand and yell obscenities at it until I feel better. It might be five seconds or five minutes. I don't know.

There's a tap on my window and I jump. I'm so on edge my teeth are grinding. Outside the foggy glass I see Violet's frail and sunken face. I get out and grab the duffel out of the trunk.

"What are you doing here, Violet?" I try to keep any emotion out of my voice.

"Garrett told me you'd be here. He told me you want out."

"Yeah, so? Of course I want out." I point to the duffel. "I can get locked up for real this time. Why the fuck wouldn't I want out? I hate this. I fucking hate it."

Violet stops me with a hand on my chest. She raises her other hand to my face and strokes my cheek.

"It's that girl, isn't it?"

I ignore her and try to step around her, but she won't let go of me.

"I loved you too, you know." Her voice is hoarse. Her words hit me hard, but I don't know how to deal with it. I laugh at how fucking stupid I am and try to move around her again. She stops me. I hope she doesn't think I was laughing at her.

Her expression doesn't change. She still looks blank, but there's sadness in her eyes.

"Just because you don't know what love looks like, doesn't mean people can't love you, Lannie."

I see flashes from the past, chunks of time spent with Violet. How she was shy and hesitant, how I craved her. How she would be everywhere I was. The way she would kiss me wildly like there was no one else. The way she would reach out to me when I was angry but I wouldn't let her in.

I place my hand over Violet's, still on my chest.

"I'm sorry, Violet," I say and mean it. With everything I have, I mean it. "I didn't realize..."

She smiles a small it's-too-late-but-thanks kind of smile. Then her face goes serious. She takes my hand and presses something into it. It's cold and sharp, and I know what it is before I look down.

"I don't need a blade, Violet. Don't be ridiculous." I try to give her back the switchblade but she won't take it.

"No Lannie, this isn't a run." The sadness is back in her eyes and she touches my face again. "You want out. They don't let people out. This is a trap. Please take the blade. I'm scared of what they're going to do to you."

I suck in a deep breath, and I'm surprised I'm not as freaked about this as I should be.

"What do you mean a trap?"

Violet sighs. "I've seen it before. It's different for everyone but it always gets out of control. They always go too far."

"What are they going to do to me, Violet?"

She's crying and shaking her head.

"I don't know. That's why I came. I don't

know, but I wanted to warn you."

"What good does that do? If I run away they will just hunt me down. I can't do anything about it."

"But they are going to hurt you. If you can fight back..." Her voice falters, and her head hangs. I put my hand on her shoulder.

"I'm done with fighting. They can't do anything worse to me than I've already been through."

Violet smiles sympathetically, "I guess not."

I place the knife back in her hand and close her fingers around it. My hands are shaking, but I believe my words. I'm terrified, but I'm tired of fighting. I'm tired of hurting. I want to be done with all of this. Not for Talia. For me.

It just took falling for Talia for me to see that.

"They've never killed anyone before, right?" I ask with a shaky voice. Violet shakes her head.

"No."

"Then I can handle whatever they do to me. Thank you, Violet. Thank you for caring about me when I obviously couldn't do the same for you."

She wraps her arms around my neck and grabs a fistful of my hair. I hug her back briefly before letting go.

"Be careful, Lannie."

I nod and turn. My legs are weak but my determination is strong. I will end this. I have to.

Violet's gone before I step through the huge metal doors of the warehouse.

The first hit is to my gut and it steals every molecule of breath I have. I fall to my knees and the duffel bag hits the ground. The second hit is to the shoulder, and I slump forward, leaning on my one good hand. The kicks start. Hammering my ribs, my legs, my arms.

I should be crying out, or fighting back, but I don't.

I think they'll never stop when someone yells. I roll over gasping for air. The room is dark and stale smelling. A shadow hovers over me. I blink hard through the pain in my ribs.

"You don't get to choose when you stop running for us, kid. I don't give a shit if you're 18 now. You're done when I say you're done." The voice is one I've never heard before. It's low and scratchy and speaks with such authority I am convinced it's the dealer.

There is a loud thud as the shadow drops something on the ground next to me. My head lolls to the side and through the darkness I see the duffel bag.

"I need you to do something for me," the shadow says.

He takes a step back and I hear the door open.

"You'll get your instructions soon. Do this one right, kid, and you get your out. Fuck it up and I'll come after you again."

CHAPTER TWENTY SEVEN
Talia

I already know this is going to be the worst weekend ever. I am two stupid romance movies into Friday night and have a bucket of ice cream on my lap.

My cell phone rings.

"'ello?" The frozen ice cream still in my mouth.

"Talia, honey?" It's Mom. I swallow hard and my brain is frozen solid.

"Mom? Hey, what's wrong?"

"Nothing's wrong. But I need you to do something for me, please. And I need you not to freak out, okay?"

My heart is thundering. Telling someone to not freak out means it is probably worth freaking out over.

"What Mom? I promise." She should know I can't promise that.

"You can't go tonight because visiting hours are over, but I got a call from your

Grandmother." Her voice trails off as the white noise in my brain takes over. I hear static but I see Nan. I haven't been to see her all week because I've been trying to sort out my head. Everything with Lachlan and Janna and even Nan has me all turned upside down and I just need to think. I can't handle seeing her like a shell of her past self. I need the strong Nan. Now I wish I would have gone to her. Maybe she needed me? Why do I keep failing the people I care about the most?

"Talia?" Mom yells. "You're not freaking out are you?"

"No, not freaking," I lie.

"So you'll go by tomorrow then? No freaking out, honey. I'll see you Monday. Your father says hi."

"Of course, Mom. I'll go in the morning." I try to keep my voice even, but I don't remember what she said to me. I can't ask though, because she'll know I went into panic mode. She doesn't sound upset. But that doesn't mean much. My mother is an expert at pleasantries.

I hang up and barely have a second to think when the doorbell rings. I'm not expecting anyone and I know it sounds stupid, but I get scared when I'm home alone. I slept in my parent's bed for most of the week.

Putting the half melted ice cream on the coffee table I look out the window, but I can't see who is on the porch. I put my eye to the peephole and my heart seizes. I can't see his face because he's hunched over but I know those curls anywhere.

I throw open the door and his body comes crashing down onto me. My legs buckle under his weight and we both go down.

"Lachlan?" I'm scared for completely different reasons now and try to lift his head with my shoulder. The cold air blows in from outside and small pile of snow is forming on the front mat. Finally, I put my weight behind it and heave Lachlan back so he's on his knees, sitting on his heels. He wheezes and all my insides contract. His breath is shallow and sounds painful but other than that I can't see anything wrong with him. No blood, no black eyes, no bruises I can see but he definitely had the crap kicked out of him. His broken hand is held to his chest. His eyes are unfocused and he's mumbling something I can't understand.

I reach across him and throw the door closed, shutting out the cold. My hands find his face and he winces. The pain brings him back and his eyes are suddenly ablaze. He's afraid.

"Talia," he breathes and takes my hand off

his face.

"What happened to you? Who did this?" I ask, my own fear turning to anger as I think of Deacon.

"I'm out...kind of," he whispers like it hurts to talk.

I move closer to him so our knees are touching, squeezing his hand in mine.

"What? Out of what?" That's what he was mumbling before, and I still don't know what it means.

He pulls his hand from mine, grabs the back of my neck and kisses me. I put my hands on his waist and pull away. I'm about to ask what the hell is going on, but I'm distracted by something warm and sticky on his side. When I take my hand away it's wet with blood.

"Lachlan?" I stand up so fast I get dizzy. "You're bleeding. I'm calling an Ambulance."

He takes my hand and pulls me abruptly back down. He squints at my hand then at his side.

"Just a scratch." He laughs but it turns into a cough. I reach down and pull him to his feet. In panic mode I'm a lot stronger than I look, and I manage to get him up the stairs to my parent's bathroom. It's bigger than mine.

Lachlan's sitting on the side of the tub, surrounded by my mom's candles and scented soaps. The sight is ridiculous. I shake my head. I have to focus and find out what happened.

I kneel in front of him and touch his side again, pulling back with more blood on my hand. I search frantically around the room for something to stop the bleeding but all my mom's towels are freaking white.

"Use my shirt," Lachlan says and my gaze is back on him. For a fraction of a second I get nervous about taking off his shirt but then I'm plunged back into panic. I grab the hem and pull it carefully over his head. He winces and coughs when he lifts his shoulder but a tiny smile forms at the corner of his mouth.

"Didn't think this was the way you'd get me naked, hey?"

I press his shirt against the cut on his side. He was right. It's not as bad as I thought. Just a scratch.

I try to smile back at him, but I'm trembling so bad I can't force any muscles to cooperate with me. I trail my shaking fingers lightly down a bruise on his stomach. My other hand is still pressing the bloody shirt to his side.

"Tell me what happened, Lachlan. Please?" I plead and he wraps his arm around me, trailing his own shaking fingers down my spine. I shiver and lean into him so my forehead rests on his bare chest.

"I wanted out. Apparently that's not going to happen yet. Apparently I have really shitty timing." He laughs, but it makes him cough again and my forehead bounces against his smooth skin with each spasm. I pull back to look at him. He's serious.

"So they beat the shit out of you?" My voice is high and uneven. "And what does that have to do with timing?"

"It's a warning, I guess. It's no big deal, really."

I practically jump to my feet. "No big deal? You could have a concussion. You could have broken ribs. They could have killed you."

I'm yelling at him, but my voice gets softer as he runs his hand up my leg and over my butt until his fingers slide under my tank top and grip my hip. I'm stunned silent, mostly because it feels so good. Now is not the time for good feelings. He pulls me close and presses his lips to my stomach over the material first then slides it up with his finger and kisses my bare skin.

I forget what I was talking about.

I tangle both my hands in his hair and he leans his cheek against my skin. I stand still and run my hands through his hair while he leans on me.

"If I didn't know any better, Hat Girl, I'd

say you've fallen for me." He chuckles and my heart starts whizzing around in my chest.

I have, but I don't say anything. I also broke up with him less than a week ago.

His head angles up to catch my eyes, and he rests his chin just above the waistband of my sweats.

"Thank you." He leans back and lowers himself into the tub, and I frown. My heart's still whirring, and I can't stop my eyes from looking at every inch of him. I didn't realize how far onto his chest and back his tattoos went. I can see the scars too. I see them under the colors permanently emblazoned on his skin.

"For what?" I ask, sitting on the edge of the cold porcelain.

"For everything," he takes my hand and plays with each one of my fingers separately.

I climb into the tub, straddling his hips and lowering myself carefully so I don't hurt him. He pulls me close and buries his head in my hair. I can feel his breath on my neck, and I'm consumed by such an intense urge that I gasp without realizing it. I breathe hard, and he pulls away to scan my face with his memorizing stare. I have no idea where I get the nerve from, not to mention totally inappropriate time and place, but I reach down and pull the tank top I'm wearing over my head.

Lachlan leans back. He's shocked. His eyes are wide but he puts his hand on my stomach.

"Talia," he starts, his eyes scanning me in a way that makes me feel beautiful, in a way that makes me feel like I'm perfect.

I shush him.

"I want you," I whisper and I do. I want him with every ounce of who I am. My skin aches to have him touch it. My eyes want to take him in, scars and tattoos and broken bones. My hands want to know what every part of him feels like. I'm consumed by him, and while I'm scared and unsure and I don't know what will happen tomorrow, right now, in this second, he's all that matters. He needs to know. I could have lost him. He needs to know what he does to me.

He reaches into his back pocket and pulls out his wallet, setting it on the side of the tub.

"Are you sure?" he asks.

"Only if you have protection." I'm shocked I don't blush.

He looks at his wallet, and I flip it open pulling out the small square package. I turn it over in my fingers and set it down on the edge of the tub.

"I'm sure."

He sits up and my arms wrap around his

neck. His shaking hands touch my sides, tentatively. The rough plaster of the cast scratches on my bare skin. He runs his thumb over the underwire of my bra then slides his good hand up, in between my breasts, and cups my neck in his hand. I lean down and take his bottom lip into my mouth, biting down lightly.

He pulls away sharply and glances toward the door.

"What's wrong?" I ask.

"I want to do this right." He takes and deep breath and starts to lift his body out of the tub. It forces me to have to get out too.

I try to help him but he won't let me so I stand still in the middle of the room, not really sure what to do. There's a bruise starting to form on his ribs just beneath a tattoo on his shoulder blade of shredded skin with fan blades under it. There are flames devouring the blades as they spin scattering ash and embers across to the other shoulder. The blades look real. Like they're really moving. I wonder why a ceiling fan?

I reach out and run my hand along it. I can't stop myself.

He spins to face me, swiping the condom off the ledge of the tub and tucking it into his back pocket. The action makes me jump. This is really going to happen.

"They're so beautiful." I run my hand down his arm.

"You're beautiful." His gaze is intense. I feel like he's trying to memorize me.

His hand is in my hair. He pulls me close and I have to stand on my toes to kiss him.

The feeling that overtakes me is like a panic attack. Quick breath. Pounding heart. Spinning thoughts. But it's good. It's all so good.

This is going to happen. I want this to happen.

He trails his finger down my spine and I bite harder on his lip in response.

He flicks the clasp of my bra. The straps slide off my shoulders and my hands instinctually go to hold the cups in place.

Okay, now I'm not so sure. Everything is racing and I don't know how to stop it. Lachlan cups the back of my neck again and pulls back to meet my wide stare. He touches his nose to mine.

"You okay?" he whispers.

I take a couple deep breaths but it doesn't stop the blood from crashing through my veins.

"We can stop," he continues, kissing my nose but never taking his eyes off me. "We can stop at anytime, Talia."

I shake my head and take my hands from

my chest. My bra falls to the floor. I should feel exposed. But for some reason I feel braver. Maybe it's the way he's looking at me like there is nothing else in the room. Maybe it's the way he mutters "holy fuck" under his breath when I hook my fingers into the waist of his jeans and pull him toward me. Maybe it has nothing to do with him and everything to do with me. All I know is that I'm ready. For him. For this. I've never been more sure of anything. It's a strange feeling. Confidence.

Lachlan's guiding me backwards, my arms are around his neck, and my feet barely touch the ground. I run into something soft and look behind me.

"My parents bed?"

He kisses me.

"Right now, I don't really care who's bed it is. I just care about you. Right now. Here with me. Nothing else matters."

He uses his body to press me back onto the soft mattress and slides his hand down my stomach toward my sweats.

CHAPTER TWENTY EIGHT
Lachlan

I have no idea what time it is. Late. I'm sitting on the couch with her head in my lap, making circles on her shoulder with my finger. The movie is over but she's still sleeping and I don't have the heart to move her. She's drooled on my jeans and I smile knowing she'll be embarrassed when she wakes up, completely forgetting that I just saw her totally naked and had her tongue as well as many other parts of her in my mouth.

She rolls over and wraps her arms around my waist, making a faint humming noise. I wince and suck air through my teeth. Her eyes shoot open and she sits up.

"I'm so sorry." Her eyes are wide, but unfocused like she is still kind of asleep and her hair is tangled on the one side. I take her shoulder and gently pull her back down.

"It's fine." It's so easy to forget with her. Forget all the things in my life that have brought me to this point. All the mistakes I've made, the disappointment I've been to those I care about the most. Now I've added her to that list.

It's not fair to her.

I want to forget, but first I have to let her in.

She's on her back, taking me in with those blue eyes. I rest my hand on her stomach, and she laces her fingers with mine. I used to think holding hands was cheesy and needy but I'm not sure anymore.

"What are you thinking about?" she asks and I smile. How girly.

I look at my cast and wiggle my fingers. I sigh.

It's time. It has to be. No one else will understand like her. I know that now.

"These," I stutter and have to take a breath. I stick out my arm. She quickly sits up and runs her fingers along my tattoos.

"These scars. They aren't all from my dad."

I said it. A tiny fraction of the weight that crushed my chest lifts. It's like opening a window on a hot day. Just a little breeze. Just a little comfort.

"Oh?" Talia wasn't expecting that.

"After a while, the pain became a way to cope. If I focused on the physical pain, the rest would go away. The numbness would fade. I started burning myself the way he burned me."

Talia's eyes get wide and I look away. I can't bear to see her judge me. Like I judge myself.

"It made me feel alive. The pain would flood me with feeling. I had shut down. When I wanted to stop, I couldn't. When I cut my wrist, I wasn't trying to kill myself. I was just trying to make the pain go away. Even if just for a little while. I was fourteen. It was before the drugs, before this..." I gesture widely meaning the drop and the beating and all the shit I've gotten myself into.

I'm silent for a long time, only the sound of my thundering heart in my ears. I feel a little better now, but I still can't look at Talia. I'm still afraid of her reaction. I half expect her to kick me out.

She doesn't. She rubs my arm. That's all. But it makes all the difference in the world. The touch doesn't feel condescending. It doesn't feel forced. It feels like Talia.

When I get the courage to face her, her eyes are soft. She looks concerned, but she doesn't pity me.

I don't know why I thought she would run screaming. I don't know why I thought the world would implode if I ever let those words escape me.

Talia climbs onto me and rests her head on my chest. I wrap my arms around her shoulders. She'll realize one day how bad I am for her, but for now I am going to take any touch from her I can get. She sighs.

"My parents didn't know how to deal with my attacks. They put me on medication when I was nine," she says and looks up at me. I feel her breath on my face.

"I know it's hard to believe people when they say they know how you feel, and I don't really know how you feel. But, I know the numbness. I know what it's like to feel nothing and everything at the same time. I also know what it's like to finally find someone who believes in you."

"Gram," I whisper and Talia squeezes my hand.

"You love her." It's a statement. It's obvious. Every good thing in my life is because of Gram.

"More than anything."

Talia sits back. She won't meet my eyes. "But I meant me. That I believe in you."

Her words are barely a whisper, but they mean everything. I'm not sure I believe it yet, but God do I want to. I pull her closer to me. I kiss her. It makes me happy and I smile against her lips. She pulls away.

"What?"

"So are we still broken-up?" I laugh. What a stupid word. Broken-up. Talia and I have been broken since the beginning, since before each other.

Her cheeks turn bright red and her chin trembles, just like the first time I kissed her. I pull her back into me before she implodes.

When she finally pulls away I stand. I am going to be really stiff but I don't think anything is broken, and I remember where and who I am, so no concussion. She stands still by the couch and watches me. The air is thickening. I can see her thinking. Her eyes move back and forth like she's watching a tennis match.

"Well, I suppose I should get home." I hook my thumb into my back pocket. My casted hand hangs at my side. I suddenly feel awkward.

Talia shifts her eyes and nods her head. I turn to walk to the entrance assuming she'll follow me.

"Stay," she says abruptly and I spin to face her. She looks down again.

"Stay?" Now I'm nervous. I clear my throat. I've never stayed before.

"Stay," she says again, this time her eyes are burning into me. She's uncertain, but so am I. She grips her elbows across her stomach as if protecting herself if I say no.

"Your parents?"
"Not home until Monday."
"Are you sure?"
She nods and walks over to me, taking my hand. My heart jumps.
Oh fuck.
I love this girl.

CHAPTER TWENTY NINE
Talia

I smile wide as Lachlan sleeps next to me. I've never had anyone sleep in my bed with me except Janna. Even then I'd end up sleeping on the floor because I'd wake up and have panic attacks or night terrors and flail until I hurt her. This morning I feel calm. It feels comfortable to have him with me. I didn't dream at all.

Nan would be proud.

I sit straight up in bed.

Nan.

"Shit!" I yell and hit the comforter with my fists. My eyes well with tears.

Lachlan rolls over and looks at me, his one eyebrow raised.

"What's wrong?"

I rush around my room getting dressed so fast I put my shirt on inside out, twice. I throw the shirt on the bed and tears roll down my cheeks. Lachlan presses his lips together. He gets out of bed and grabs my shoulders, his cast scratching my skin.

"Talia?"

"I was supposed to go see her." I'm full out crying

275

now, standing in my room with only a bra and jeans on while my boxer-clad kind-of boyfriend looks at me like I'm crazy.

"When were you supposed to go see her?" he asks.

"This morning."

Lachlan scrunches his face and glances at the clock beside my bed. It's 3:00.

"But," he starts and then stops to think. I know he thinks I am a big baby when it comes to Nan, but I'm glad he doesn't look judge-y.

"Let me drive you." Lachlan's voice is even and he rubs my shoulders.

"I have my parent's car." I pull my shirt over my head and he stops me again, wrapping his arms around my shoulders. I hug him back, my tears sliding on his bare chest. My hands slide up his back and grip his shoulders. I feel like I could touch him forever and never get sick of it, but for now I have to go.

"I want to drive you. You're not really in the right state of mind," he says. He has a point. I nod and kiss him fast on the cheek.

~

I stand at the door to the hospital room, afraid to open it. I'm afraid of what I'll see and my thoughts buzz around the worst things that could have happened. She can't be dead. I know that for sure. My mom would have come home for that. But the negative thoughts press in. I see Nan's frail body, pale skin and bald head. I hear her raspy breaths and tired voice. I smell the sickness and antiseptic. I feel her calloused skin.

An arm slips around my waist and Lachlan kisses the back of my neck protectively.

"It'll be okay, Talia. She isn't going to be mad at you."

I'm not so sure. I place a shaking hand on the doorknob and push it open slowly.

Nan is sitting on her bed, cross-legged, playing cards. She's in a gown like usual and wearing the hat I made. Her cheeks are a little more flush and her eyes are a little brighter. She smiles a real authentic Nan smile. I just about burst out crying with all the emotion that floods my body. I'm wracked by guilt that I haven't been to see her in so long and all the while she was getting better.

"Tali, darling. I was wondering when I'd see you." She smiles wider when she sees Lachlan behind me. "I sure hope you kids used protection."

Nan winks at Lachlan, and I stumble backwards into him. He's laughing when he catches me and keeps me up on my feet, which are on fire along with the rest of my body.

"I'll be in the car," Lachlan whispers in my ear and it sends a shiver down me, which embarrasses me even further.

Nan has a big grin on her face. "That will teach you for forgetting your Nan for a boy."

She winks at me this time because Lachlan is gone. Tears fill my eyes and Nan laughs.

"I'm only teasing. Come here beautiful!" She opens her arms and I crash into her, not thinking about how frail she still might be.

I'm crying but laughing at the same time. I really

wish I could get a handle on these tears some day.

"But mom called, said not to freak out, said to check on you, I forgot."

Nan is stroking my hair and laughing.

"What a terrible child I have. I'm sure you freaked out too."

I nod and sit up.

"Well not all news is devastating. This time the news is good. I'm done my first round of treatment. So we have to wait a little bit, and I'll get another scan to see if it's gone."

I cry harder and throw my arms around her again.

"I'm not out of the fog yet. I will still have another round of treatments, but if the spot shrunk my odds are better."

I squeeze her and try to pass every good feeling and happy thought I have through it because I can't find my voice.

"That's why I wanted you to come in, but I guess you were busy." Her eyebrows are pulled together but she's smiling. Her voice is playful.

I blush again. "Sorry Nan."

She takes my hand in hers and squeezes it.

"Don't you be sorry. You need to stop fussing over me so much. I'm an old lady. I've lived a long time, and I don't need you fussing. You're young. You should be out having fun. But I thought you two broke up?"

"We did."

"Because he beat up some boy you used to date?"

I opened my mouth twice before sound came out. "How did you know about that?"

"I hear things." She raises her eyebrow. "Plus while you're out gallivanting with the neighborhood boys, Georgina has her eyes and ears out for me."

Of course.

"Speaking of Georgina, she told me that Greta approached her about the Charity Drive. Do you want to talk about that?"

I roll my eyes.

"She's evil, that woman. She wants to ban the group because she doesn't like Lachlan."

Nan nods but she frowns.

"Greta told Georgina that she wants you to back out of the Drive. She's fine with the rest of the ladies carrying on as normal."

I start to shake, Deacon didn't tell me that. Just me? I think back to when Deacon told me. He said you... I just assumed he meant all of us.

"Me? But I was juried in."

Nan shrugs. "I don't know, darling, but she really doesn't want you to be involved. She can't force you out, but I just want to let you know that Georgina will be talking to you about it today."

"What should I do?" I start to chew on my finger and pull it out of my mouth. I can't have a panic attack. I've just started to believe I can get them under control.

"I don't know. I can't help you with this one. You have to do what you think is right."

~

I'm a thick black cloud of hate by the time I leave the hospital. My bones ache because my muscles are so tense and my arms are swinging violently. After everything that's happened with Deacon, Janna, and Lachlan, this is the moment I decide to lose it.

Okay, I am not really deciding to lose it, the fiery rage that rips through me is deciding. I wonder if this is how Lachlan feels when he gets mad. I feel like I'll explode if I don't get it out.

Lachlan gets out of Georgina's car, all happy looking. He notices quickly and the smile falls from his face. Now he's walking toward me, concerned.

"What's wrong? What happened?"

I can't keep it in anymore and I drop my bag on the ground and I let it all bubble over.

"What's wrong?" I yell throwing my arms out. Lachlan looks confused.

"That stupid fucking bitch is what's wrong." The words feel sharp on my tongue. I never swear because I think it's mostly unnecessary but it feels so good to say it. Lachlan seems more confused than ever.

"She wants me out. Me! That uppity snob and her douchebag grandson want me out of the Charity Drive. I thought it was all of us. But no. Just me."

Lachlan tries to touch my face, and I push his hand away.

"No, No I am so sick of people treating me like I'm a baby. I am so fucking sick of deserving to be treated that way." I laugh and Lachlan smirks.

"You know what?" I continue pointing in his face, his smile across his whole face now. "I'm going to have my own sale."

I put my hands on my hips and nod my head. Lachlan's laughing.

"I'm going to sell my own hats. On my own. Then I'll give the money to the Shelter as a big fat go fuck yourself."

I let out a huge breath and Lachlan steps up to me. I feel a thousand, no a million, times better. I feel hands on my hips and Lachlan draws my body into his.

"God, I love you." He kisses me hard but I'm stunned. Frozen in time, my lips refuse to move while my brain catches up.

Um, what?

I stare at him. How is it that I have the biggest meltdown ever and swear more in two minutes than I have in my entire life and still it's Lachlan with the shock value.

He runs his thumb over my bottom lip that is hanging open, I'm sure of it. He lightly presses my jaw closed and kisses me again.

CHAPTER THIRTY

Lachlan

When I drop Talia off at her meeting she's still on about how she's going to stick it to Deacon's grandmother. I'm all for it, and I think Talia's super hot when she's pissed at someone other than me. She turns to me with her hand on the door handle.

"Come in? I know you were booted from the team but I want you here," she says. I see that I don't get a choice. It is phrased as a question but I know Gram well enough to recognize rhetorical.

I shut the car off and get out just as my cell phone buzzes. Talia's face slackens and her eyes get big. My whole body tenses. We stare at each other over the car, both very aware of what this means.

"Don't go. What are they going to do? Just don't go. My dad's a lawyer. I'll get him to help you."

I know it's desperate, but I want to believe

her. I start to pull my hand out of my pocket. I can't just not go.

"You don't understand, Tali. I have to do this. Just this once and I'll be done."

"How do you know? How do you know they won't just keep calling you, or coming after you? How do you know it's over if you jump every time they call."

"Because if I don't they'll do more than just 'beat me up'" I mock her and I see the hurt in her eyes but she needs to understand.

"Why do you do that, Lachlan? Why do you act like you're the only person in the world who has ever felt pain? Why do you always think you are the only one who can help you?"

That's not true. But I don't tell her that. What I say is entirely the wrong stupid thing to say.

"You think because you're going to stand up to one old woman that you can solve my problems?"

I shouldn't have said that. Her expression of disappointment confirms that I shouldn't have said that.

"Call me later so I know you're okay." Then she turns and walks away.

I am such a fucking moron. Why did I say that?

I watch her until she disappears into the

wool shop then pull out my phone.

It's a new address. One I've never run to before. This doesn't feel right.

Of course it doesn't. The dealer doesn't meet with a runner if it's not important. Dangerous.

I see her through the big storefront window. Hugging Gram. My heart skips. I should listen to her. I should run after her and say sorry for the millionth time. I should help her plan her ridiculous coup of the Charity Drive. But the dealer said he'd go after her. I don't think he would. I am pretty sure it was just a threat to make sure I do this drop, but I would rather her be pissed at me than in danger. Any day.

I get into Grams car and drive away.

~

The ride is silent, just the rumble of the engine as I drive to the drop. I park quite far away and as I walk in broad daylight to the drop site I wonder why this isn't happening at night. Most runs happen at night, and this one feels off. Especially because of the size of the bag and the shady-ness of the house I'm standing in front of. It's ten times creepier than Garret's.

The thought makes my stomach tighten and my steps get slower and the crunching of the snow under my feet gets louder. I should just turn and walk away. Talia's right, what are they going to do? They wouldn't kill me. I laugh. This isn't a fucking movie. It's not like they're a gang. I still can't shake the thought that something is off when I approach the door. It's open, just a little, and I try to peer inside. It's dark. And quiet.

Too quiet.

My heart starts up, burning blood at such a speed it makes me dizzy. This dread feels familiar and I stand silently in front of the door trying to place it. I've been here before. Standing on the other side, kicking myself for not making the right choice. Here I am again, but this time I'm not 15. This time I'm not just some misguided kid. I should've known better.

Fuck.

Pushing the door open with my foot, I drop the duffel on the ground and put my hands in the air before the cop with the gun pointed in my face has a chance to say anything.

CHAPTER THIRTY ONE

Talia

"I'm not sure that's such a great idea, dear," Georgina says. I clench my fist in my lap. I knew she wouldn't like this plan for revolution I have blazing through my mind, and true I really haven't given it enough thought yet but I'm excited. I want to *do* something. The Charity Drive isn't about appearances or reputations. It's about helping people.

"But, Georgina, she thinks she can wear her thousand dollar business suit and give a few bucks to the homeless. That's helping them? It's garbage and you know it. They don't even give *all* the money to the shelter." My voice is raised to a level that annoys even me.

"The Drive has costs, too, you know. They do the best they can."

I snort.

"Nan told me they pay her. That's she's not

even doing it on volunteer. She's some sort of party planner and they pay her to organize."

Georgina leans back in her chair and rubs her shoulder.

"You okay?"

"Oh I'm fine dear, just stiff today. Well if you want to stick it to the man, that's great Talia, but I will sit this one out. I'm too old for this."

She smiles, but it only moves half of her mouth. I glance over my shoulder to the door. Lachlan should be here by now. I'm worried about him but I can't say anything to Georgina.

"Do you want me to give you a ride home? I'm not sure Lachlan's coming."

I look back to her and she's looking at me but her eyes are empty. She isn't focusing.

"I'm telling you, Nancy." Georgina's voice is angry. "I'm telling you now to get out. For the boy. You must protect him no matter what."

I slide back in my chair and gape at her.

"Georgina?" I reach out my hand and she doesn't move. The side of her mouth is drooping and she still won't focus. I shake her hand and it falls off her knee.

Something's wrong. Very wrong.

I move my head frantically, but everyone has gone. The meeting's over and everyone's gone.

I fumble for my cell phone in my huge bag but can't find it under the yarn. Georgina speaks again but this time it doesn't make sense. The sounds she makes aren't even words but she is looking at me now.

My hands shake violently and thoughts start swirling around my mind.

Don't panic. Don't panic.

I scan the shop again, as if someone would have magically appeared because I need help.

"Georgina?" I reach out to her just as a bubble of air bursts from her lungs. The sound freezes me right through every nerve and blood vessel. A vision of Janna flashes through my mind as she convulsed and foamed on the floor at the Halloween party.

I grab Georgina's shoulders and shake her. I yell her name but her face has lost all control, she's shaking and drooling and making this noise that rocks me back into focus.

I turn and run across the store. I jump over the counter, sending jewelry displays clattering to the ground. I run my shaking hands along shelf under the counter.

There's a phone here. Where is it? The phone, the phone, the... My fingers touch the cold plastic, and I rip it out of the holder. I stab out 911 and run around the counter back to Georgina.

Her eyes are wide open but not focused on anything.

I cry out at the phone just as someone answers.

"911 what's your emergency," the male voice says.

I'm stunned silent for a moment because I don't know what my emergency is. I don't know what's wrong.

"Are you still there?" the voice sounds again, and I take a huge gulp of air.

"She's, she's not responding." I say with a shaky voice.

"Not responding to what, miss?"

"Anything. Her eyes are open. She isn't focusing. She was fine. We were talking then she just started mumbling nonsense. She was fine two minutes ago."

The operator's silent for a second.

"Please tell me your location, miss. I have an ambulance on the way."

I nod, not thinking that he can't see me.

"You're location, miss."

"Um, the Wool Shop on 13th Ave. What can I do? How can I help her?"

I reach out to touch her, but pull my hand back.

"Is she breathing?"

"I don't know. I can't tell."

"Put your hand over her mouth. Can you feel air from her mouth or nose?"

I'm shaking so bad I don't think I can hold the phone with one hand but I do. I put my hand by her mouth and a sob catches in my throat.

"Oh my god, oh my god. No I can't feel it. She's not breathing."

"Do you know CPR, miss?"

"No!" I'm crying now. I pace in front of the chair and cry. The sight of Georgina crushes my heart further and further into my chest with every beat.

She's dying, and I can't help her. She's dying, and I can only watch.

"I can walk you through it, Miss. You think you can do it?"

My head swims, the panic is in the back of my mind, but like when Janna was overdosing I feel of wave of clarity pass through me. I'm aware of everything down to every single individual sweat bead that has formed on my forehead.

I nod, and then remember he can't see me.

"Yes, yes I can do it."

CHAPTER THIRTY TWO

Lachlan

I'm sitting in the dirt outside of a rundown shit-hole in the worst area of town, and I've run my hand through my hair so many times I have snow on my face and dirt in my mouth. My body shakes and I can't stand yet. I'm still in utter shock of how a gun pointed in my face ends up with me, uncuffed, sitting in the snow, totally free.

I know how it happened, but I'm shocked. When I stop being shocked I know I'm going to be pissed. Those fucking assholes set me up. They set me up, to set up the cops and now everyone is busted. The duffel was full of nothing. Plastic bags inside plastic bags then taped together to look like bricks of pot. They knew I wouldn't look in the bag.

I'm not going to be as mad as that cop was when he found out I was just a runner. You can't arrest a guy for having a bag full of bags.

Hence why I'm sitting in the dirt, *not* arrested. I flop back into the crunchy snow, unconcerned that my ass is freezing. My ass is free. That's all that matters.

I don't know how long I lay there watching my breath freeze with every exhale.

My cell phone buzzes and my heart seizes. I pull it from my pocket but it's not from them. It's from Talia.

Meet me at the hospital now

Her words do nothing to ease the tension in my body. I sit up and read the message again. I think of her Nan and jump to my feet.

If something happened and I wasn't there.... The last words I said to her play in my head. I'm such a selfish asshole.

My near miss with the cops is pushed from my head as I run to the car. I am free now and I'm not going to fail her again.

~

I don't remember getting to hospital, or parking, or flying through the door. I don't have my first rational thought until I'm in the hallway and I see her.

Talia stands just outside her Nan's room and I can see her body shake from here. Her eyes are puffy and tears are flowing down her face faster and harder than I've ever seen before.

I hurt for her to see how much pain she's

in, and I start to walk toward her. Halfway to her, she takes a step backward and a loud sob escapes her lips. I stop, and so does my heart. My eyes flicker toward the door of her Nan's room and she shakes her head.

Her one arm is pressed to her side and she's chewing on the index finger of the other. Her eyes are glazed and the sadness in them squeezes my guts to mush. I start toward her and she sobs again taking another step back.

Why is she doing this? The last time she got bad news about her Nan she came barreling at me with the force of an entire army.

Unless.

Behind the sadness that radiates from her there's something else. Something that makes her retreat from me.

Unless it's not her Nan.

As if an icicle were plunged into my chest, a coldness slowly spreads through my body and I take a step back this time.

"I tried, Lachlan," Talia sobs.

No. The cold turns to numbness. My fingers curl into fists, but I can't feel them.

No. It can't be Gram.

"I did everything I could." I can barely understand her. I can barely hear her.

Her voice echoes through my brain

muffled by my ears, which are trying to shut her out.

Gram.

I feel hands on my face, but just the pressure. I know they're Talia's, but I can't feel the warmth. I can't feel the familiar tingle of when she touches me.

Like someone had snapped their fingers, I spring out of my hypnosis and wrap my hand around Talia's wrist.

"Where is she?"

"Lachlan, I–"

"Where is she?"

Talia looks down. "ICU," she whispers. "They have her on life support. I tried, really I did. But the damage..." She's crying again.

The foundation of my soul actually cracks. I hear and feel it push through me with such force I can't breathe.

I pull her close and press my lips to hers. I savor how soft she feels, the almond and vanilla smell of her hair, how she tastes like tears and toothpaste.

Then I pull away, turning and leaving her standing stunned in the hallway.

I barely take three steps when she calls my name. I stop but I don't turn around. I can't. If I look at her I might not have the strength to leave.

"Leaving me isn't going to make her wake

up, Lachlan." Talia's voice is just a whisper, but her words have enough power to break through the last of my soul, splitting it completely in two.

There's a gurgle that comes from my mouth as the crack moves through me, tearing me open. I think I'm going to throw up.

But I don't. Instead the crack finally hits the back of my eyes. They fill.

Gram.

The only person who was ever there for me. I wasn't there for her.

The same gurgle as before forms in my throat but this time louder. I sink to my knees and Talia is instantly at my side, wrapping her arms around me.

I sink into her and she holds me up.

I cry. No. I more than cry. I relive it. I relive every good thing Gram ever did for me and how I repaid her by lying, by sneaking around, by getting arrested again.

My shoulders are heaving and Talia is stroking my hair. She's rubbing my back. I spin to wrap my arms around her and like I did for her on the night she found out about her Nan's cancer, she pulls me into her chest and holds me as tight as she can. She presses her lips to my ear and hums. Her voice is beautiful, just like Grams. She runs her hand

through my hair and rocks back and forth.
She sings the song over and over until I stop.
Until I have nothing left. Until I am empty.

CHAPTER THIRTY THREE
Talia

Lachlan's sleeping on my couch. He's exhausted, even in sleep. It shows all over his features.

I feel like I could sleep standing up but I just watch him. I'm still rubbing his back with one hand and holding my cell in the other.

I'm on my way. I'll bring food. You need anything else?

Janna texts and I reply that we're good.

I talked to my parents and they agreed that Lachlan could stay, but I'm too shaken to cook anything, or move, or think at all.

Janna shows up an hour later with pizza and almost drops it in her haste to hug me. I assure her a thousand times that I will be okay and she eats pizza with me while Lachlan snores on the couch.

"I don't mean to bring this up now, Tal. Totally shitty timing, but I got a call from the cops yesterday," she whispers as she puts her shoes on at the front door. I groan. Not this again.

"Yeah, bad timing," I mumble.

"They told me that they need to question me further about my statement. I told them when I talk to a lawyer. I didn't know if that would work but they didn't question me." She shrugs and I can't help but smile.

"You watch too many movies."

She hugs me.

"I'm just saying because that means they might call Lachlan back in too. That poor guy. It's never just easy for him, is it?" She steals a glance at him and there is a sympathetic sadness in her eyes. I nod.

Nothing is ever easy with Lachlan.

~

Early Monday morning, Lachlan gets a call. He's eating breakfast at my kitchen table and he looks like he's going to throw up. There's a dozen yes's, and okay's and then he hangs up. I'm pacing in front of him. I want to pounce on him and ask him a ton of questions.

"That was the police department." His face is still pale and his eyes dart around nervously.

"What?"

"He said they need me to come in. You too," Lachlan's voice trails off. Janna was right. I don't have it in me right now to make a statement. Plus, Lachlan going to court over punching Deacon in the face seems just about as ridiculous as me wanting to take down Deacon's grandma and the knitting show.

"Let's go then," I say with more confidence than I even knew I had.

~

I watch Lachlan enter the station. He lacks any emotion, but not in his typical I don't care because I'm cool way. He really doesn't care. It breaks me to see him like this. This whole thing was sprung on him and I hate Deacon even more, if that's possible.

Deacon stands with a lawyer, his hand casually thrown into his suit pant pocket. He's leaning forward talking to Greta and laughing, ignoring us. She scrutinizes me. I don't like it.

Why are they even here?

My body does this spasm thing where I'm not sure if my legs are going to give out or I'm going to launch myself across the hall at her. I'm just about to decide when a warm hand slips inside of mine and squeezes. It's not Lachlan's hand. It's way too small.

I turn to Janna who is all smiles. Her grin takes up half her face. She shouldn't even be here.

"What are you doing here? Shouldn't you

be at school? And why do you look so pleased with yourself?" I mumble and she laughs.

"I brought someone. To help us. A lawyer." She sounds as proud of herself as she looks. I am just confused. She winks.

Us?

She takes a step back so I can see. Briefcase in hand, my dad is standing awkwardly behind her.

"Dad?" I'm still confused. "What are you doing here?"

My dad clears his throat. It's something he always does before addressing people professionally.

"Janna called me yesterday and told me everything." My stomach flops when he says everything and I glance sideways at Janna.

Dad says hello to Lachlan and stretches out his hand. Lachlan looks at it, and then he looks at me. His eyes say *what the hell?*

I shrug.

Lachlan smiles at my dad and shakes his hand. I let out a slow breath. Janna squeezes my hand again.

"Not really the place you want your dad to meet your boyfriend, hey Tal?" She giggles. I'm so very lost. Why is she here? Why is my dad here? And what did she mean by *everything*?

"Not exactly. What did you tell him?"

I'm distracted by Dad as he approaches Deacon's lawyer and they shake hands stiffly before my dad takes him aside. I wonder what they're talking about.

An officer comes and ushers Lachlan and my dad one way while Deacon and his lawyer go another.

I sit on a small bench in the hall and Janna sits next to me.

"I'm sorry, Tal. I hope you aren't mad at me for telling him, but I knew you wouldn't. Deacon can't get away with this. We all know that Lachlan did what he did because of me. I think Deacon lied and that's why we're being called back in."

She tucks a strand of hair behind her ear.

"This is the first time I've been asked to come in." I remember Deacon asking me whether I'd gotten called in.

"Yeah, I'm not supposed to say anything but they think Lachlan and Deacon were just fighting over you. I was brought in to make a statement about where I got drugs. And I may, or may not, have let Deacon's involvement slip." She smirks.

It's hard to cross Janna, but she's vicious if she wants to be.

"What Lachlan did wasn't right. But Deacon gets away with everything. He's such... He's such a...dick."

I laugh and nudge her with my shoulder.

"I'm glad you called my dad. He's good."

I used to go to court and watch my dad when I was a kid. I loved it. I thought he was a superhero. My superhero. Then we needed a bigger house, so he took that corporate job. Every day he became less and less interested. Every day he became more and more busy.

And not until now did I feel sorry for him. He gave up what he loved for us and all I did was resent him for it. Blame him for not being around. But our family is bigger now. Things have to change.

My eyes fill with tears and I shake my head. I really need to get this crying thing under control. But I can't help but feel happy, like truly happy. It still blows my mind. I remember I'm going to have a brother and I haven't told Janna about it yet. It will have to wait a bit longer.

Lachlan comes out with my dad. His face is white and his eyes are unfocused. My dad has his hand around Lachlan's shoulders and a smile across his face.

CHAPTER THIRTY FOUR

Lachlan

I never would ever guess that Talia's dad would help me. Dads don't help me. They warn their daughters to stay away from me.

But Malcolm's smile is genuine. When he shook my hand he looked me in the eyes.

The cop asks me the same questions they asked me the night of the party and I answered them the exact same way.

The officer's holding a paper and his eyes flick between me and whatever's written down.

I remember Deacon saying he would tell them that I hit Talia. That must be why they brought us in.

"Lachlan?" the officer says and Malcolm squeezes my shoulder.

"Sorry, what?" I shift in my seat.

"Was there anything you wanted to add to your statement?"

I shake my head.

Malcolm reaches across and shakes the officers hand.

"I'm sure you'll see that this is just a couple of young guys fighting for a girl's heart." Malcolm smiles, "That girl's sitting out in the hall should you need to obtain a statement from her."

The officer clears his throat. "I think you might be right, Mr. Gregory."

He shakes his head lightly as he shuffles his papers. Malcolm motions for me to get up. He tucks his case under one arm and throws the other one over my shoulders. It feels really strange to me. I'm not used to this. It's really messing with my mind.

He guides me out into the hall where Talia and Janna are waiting.

"I know what's behind all this, Lachlan. Janna told me everything. I trust you are turning this around now that you are officially an adult?" he says as we're walking.

I'm stunned so I stop walking. He speaks about me like it's no big deal that I have the reputation I do. He doesn't say it with pity, or distain. Just like it's a fact.

"Why are you doing this?" I don't mean for it to sound so harsh, but it does. I also didn't mean to dodge the question because I am turning it around.

"Doing what?" Malcolm's expression

TIGHT KNIT

doesn't change.

"Helping me." I can't stop myself from feeling indebted to him.

He shifts his gaze to Talia then back at me.

"I'm not." Again with the facts. "I'm helping my little girl. She sees something in you, and I trust her. I did this for her, Lachlan. Not for you."

I feel relief but also a little dejected at the same time.

"Don't get me wrong, I think you're a nice kid and I understand your situation so I'm willing to give you a little leeway. I'm not huge on your reputation, or sleeping at my house alone with my daughter. But I trust her. She wouldn't have asked Rebecca and me for you to stay if it wasn't important."

I blush. He doesn't know what we did in his bedroom. I look down, letting my hair fall in my face to hide my heated cheeks. I never blush. Damn this girl.

"Thanks," I mumble. It's not a word I use often. "For everything. She deserves."

That's when I feel her. Her body slams into mine, and I scoop her up with my good arm. She kisses my neck, my ear, my jaw, my cheek then my lips. I set her down and press her head into my chest. I'm uncomfortable kissing her with her dad watching me.

Talia pulls away from me and pounces on

305

Malcolm.

"Dad." She throws her arms around his neck and he sets down his case so he can hug her.

"Dad, thank you so much. You have no idea how much this means to me."

Malcolm kisses the top of her head. "You know I'd do anything for you, Tali. Anything."

"Do I need to go in there?" She asks, chewing on her finger.

"Maybe, but not today." He hugs her again and then takes a step back.

I'm so glad because I need to get out of this place, and I'm still totally not used to all this love-y shit going around.

"I think tonight would be a good night for takeout," Malcolm says. "You in?"

Talia and Janna nod. I don't know what to do. I still can't go home. But I'm not sure if the invitation extends to me.

Talia grabs my hand, pulling me from my thoughts of Gram.

"You coming?"

I smile.

"Yeah, I'm right behind you. The view is better from back here anyway." I try to make things sound like before. I need to feel like I did before. Happy. With her.

I wink at her and she blushes, glancing to make sure Malcolm didn't hear.

She hits my chest.
"You are so bad."
"You have no idea."

CHAPTER THIRTY FIVE

Talia

Sitting with Nan by her hospital bed is almost back to normal. Well as normal as hanging out in a hospital can be. We knit together while she hums with the soft sounds of the TV in the background.

Pain stabs through my heart as I watch Nan. I thought I was going to lose her. I still might. But the thought never crossed my mind that it might be Georgina I'd lose first. I feel the pain in Lachlan's eyes again. I left him in front of Georgina's room.

Today's the day they take her off life support.

His aunts and uncles are here, and they even let his mom come and say goodbye a few days ago. I was here for him then too.

"Can you find your way back, darling?" Nan's voice sounds like it used to. Like honey and soft towels and sunny bright skies and everything else I love in this world.

"Hmm?" I look up and my eyebrows pull together.

"You seemed lost in your thoughts."

She continues to hum, wrapping the yarn around the needles.

"I'm just worried about Lachlan. He's still really torn up."

"Well of course he is. What a horrible thing to experience after everything he's been through already."

I nod, but Nan doesn't see me.

"He'll pull through. He's strong that one. And stubborn too." Nan smiles. There is something behind the smile I don't recognize. Her eyes sparkle and get that glazed stare girls get when they think about someone they like.

I roll my eyes.

"Do you have a crush on my boyfriend, Nan?"

She smiles wider. "I just might. He is so handsome, just like your pops."

"Well hands off." I tap her leg with my knitting needle.

Lachlan sticks his head through the door.

"My Aunt wants to take me to dinner," he says and steps in the room. I don't think he's been crying. I'm not sure if that is good or bad yet. He seems okay, sad and tired, but okay.

Nan makes him hug her and he looks so awkward.

"Come with me?" he asks, then stops me when I start to protest. "I need you to come with me. I need your help to get through this."

He stumbles over the words a little but by the crooked half smile he knows he has me. I did after all try to force him to accept my help and then got mad when he refused. Multiple times. I can't turn him down the first time he actually asks for it.

"Are you two going to at least stop by the Drive tomorrow?"

I had totally forgotten about that. I've been so focused on Lachlan and helping him pack up Georgina's stuff, get the house ready for the funeral and prepare for his aunts that I totally pushed the Charity Drive from my mind.

"I don't think I want to go."

"I feel bad Talia, that you worked so hard just to be left out like that. If I wasn't sick I'd march straight up to that Greta woman and give her a piece of my mind."

I laugh. That would be a sight.

Kissing Nan on the forehead I say, "The Drive will do just fine without me, Nan. That doesn't matter right now. I have everything I need right here."

Nan smiles. "I am so proud of you, darling."

Before I can answer Lachlan slips his hand into mine and pulls me out the door.

~

The first weekend of Christmas break I get a phone call telling me to get dressed and get outside. Lachlan has a surprise for me. He made me keep my eyes closed the whole time. He even pulled my wool hat over my face for good measure.

His hands are over my eyes now and the wool gloves I knit him are tickling my eyelashes. I feel the pressure of his body against mine, but it's cold outside so all I hear is the cracking of our winter coats as they rub together.

"Where are you taking me?" I ask for the tenth time.

I'm holding onto his forearms so I don't slip. It's so much nicer now that his cast is off. It's not supposed to be off. But Lachlan does things his own way.

"It's a secret," he whispers in my ear and kisses the back of my neck. I shiver as the air freezes the kiss on my skin.

"It's too early for secrets, Lachlan." I fight a bubbling yawn.

Lachlan laughs and tells me to put out my hands out to open a door.

I feel the smooth door even under my gloves and I push.

The door jingles. I'm hit with a blast of warm air and that smell.

I don't need eyes to know where I am.

"Why are we at the wool shop?" I wrinkle my nose and I hear laughter that makes me jump. It's not Lachlan's. It sounds like Janna.

"I told you she'd know right away," croaks another voice. Marybeth.

I try to turn to look at Lachlan, but he has me firmly pressed against him.

I feel him sigh.

"Fine, then, Tal. But way to make this totally anti-climactic."

Lachlan lifts his hands and it takes a second to adjust to the light.

The whole knitting group is here. Anna is beside her husband, Marybeth is with them and she's smiling. Marybeth. Smiling.

I must be dreaming.

Janna skips toward me and grabs my hand. She smiles a guilty smile. She knew about this. I wondered why she was being so crazy the last few weeks. Ever since the day of Georgina's Will reading, Janna has been on me like a psychopath.

I'm gaping at the wool shop. All the couches moved. In their place are long tables, filled with knitted things. Scarves, tea cozies, doilies, sweaters, mitts, everything.

But along the back wall are my hats. All of them.

How?

I focus on Janna.

"How did you?"

She giggles.

"Your mom stole them for us."

I turn to Lachlan who just leans against the wall and shrugs. He so knew.

"Why?" I stutter. "What's going on?"

I must look like an idiot, my eyes flickering from person to person.

"You wanted to stick it to that hag," Marybeth says. Anna swats her arm and Marybeth glares.

"So we pulled our booths from the show."

"Why would you do that?" That's just silly. The money goes to charity. And why did no one tell me?

"Ask, Red here." Marybeth points to Janna. "She's the brains of this outfit. We didn't want to do the show without you, kid. So we're having our own show."

Janna tucks a strand of hair behind her ear and her lips pull up into a small smile.

I turn my attention to Lachlan again, and he puts his hands up in the air.

"Don't look at me. It's all Janna. I was just the muscle." He winks and my heart flutters.

I love him.

I love Janna.

The only thing that would make this more perfect is Nan.

Lachlan must see it in my face because he holds his cell phone up. In a little speech bubble it says,

Thanks son, Becca and I will be there soon. We'll pick up Florence on the way. This will mean a lot to her. We appreciate you doing this.

Becca is my mom. This must be a text from my dad.

Why is my dad texting my boyfriend? My heart jumps. He called Lachlan son. That makes me panic a little.

Pick up Florence. Mean a lot to her. Me? Or Nan. Nan's coming.

"But?" I start and Lachlan laughs at my confusion.

"How did you...? Isn't she?"

Lachlan's smile turns into a grin, "Baby, com'on. I'm charming. No one can resist a bad boy. Including nurses."

I roll my eyes.

He pulls me in and kisses me. It sucks the smart-ass comment I had brewing right out of my mouth. I melt into him. I can't help it.

He pulls back and touches his nose to mine.

"I can't stay to help with your sale," he says. "I have to go sign the papers for Gram's house. I still can't believe she left it to me."

My heart sinks a little remembering Georgina. She was amazing to leave her house and her car to Lachlan. And his aunt and uncle agreed to help him out so he could stay and finish school. They tried to get him to sell it, but he isn't ready yet. He'll come around.

"You deserve it," I say. "Go." I push him playfully and he grins.

He kisses me again quickly.

"I love you, Hat Girl."

"I love you, *Bad Boy.*" I say sarcastically.

He steps back and presses his finger to my nose.

"Now go sell some doilies, you old lady."

I roll my eyes again and watch him leave.

Janna steps up beside me and bumps me with her hip.

"The director of the shelter will be here at five, so let's get these doors open. Plus I told everyone at school to come early or their hat will be gone." She giggles.

"I can't believe you did this for me," I whisper and she throws her arm around my shoulder.

"You deserve it."

I smile.

ALLIE BRENNAN

~

Everything isn't okay yet. Nan's still sick, Janna's still working through what to do about Deacon, Lachlan's still hurting, Mom and Dad are still trying to figure out how this new arrival will affect us. But I feel good about it.

I feel like no matter what happens I can handle it. I've never felt like this before. It feels good.

UNDER THE DUSTY SKY

ALLIE BRENNAN

COMING SPRING/SUMMER 2013

CHAPTER ONE

It's been tense around the farm since my brother, Hunter, told us he was leaving. I don't think Daddy thought he was serious. But here he is, his suitcase packed and Emma waiting outside in his pick-up. The black one that Dad threatened to take away from him after we all realized he was *definitely* going to Lincoln. No matter what.

Hunter has these eyes that coat me in their silky brown concern. He reaches out, grabbing one of my long braids, and tugs it. Like he used to when I was a kid.

"Gracie, you know I love you." His smile is strong and masculine. He looks more like a man now. More like Dad. The sun filters through the screen door and little dust specks sparkle in the air as they float around my favorite brother. The brother that's taken care of me since I was three, since mom left.

I stick out my lip and lightly kick his foot. Hoping it will work like it used to, but my guilt trips started losing their power when I turned thirteen.

"Then don't leave me. Not with the twins." I point a thumb at my other two brothers.

Hunter takes me by the shoulders and pulls me into his chest. I squeeze his waist.

He's solid. Just as solid as Daddy, but years of hard farm work will do that.

Everyone pitches in. Daddy's motto. I even have guns from shoveling horse crap all day.

Hunter chuckles, his chest bouncing my head with each short burst. I pull away.

"Not funny, Hunt. They're lazy." I'm flat-out whining now, running out of tricks to make him stay.

The twins, standing on either side of me in our huge boot room, hit my shoulders at the same time. I glare at Hunter. He's leaving me with this.

"Hey! Don't hit your sister you little shits." He shoves each of them with one hand and they both stumble back into the wall. I smile. Hunter always protects me. I'm the youngest and the only girl. Totally unfair.

"Don't go," I whisper. I know he's going.

He looks over his shoulder out the door, and runs his hand over his short brown hair. Same color as mine.

"Graceland, you know I'm going. This is important to Emma. I love her, and you love me. So let me go, little sis."

Tears stab at the corners of my eyes. I promised I wouldn't cry. Told myself that I'd be mad at her forever. Hunter always said I was the only girl he'd ever love. Until Emma moved to town.

"Fine. Go." My mouth pulls into a full and totally fake smile. Teeth and all. I know Hunter sees through it, but it works on everyone else.

I kiss his cheek quickly and run up the stairs to the third story of our old farm house. I hate when the twins see me cry and I don't know if I can stop the tears now.

"I'll be home next weekend, Gracie. Don't be like this." He yells up the stairs.

I slam my bedroom door and sit on the floor right in front of it. The wood is cold on my bare legs, even though it's shorts weather outside already.

I don't let more than three tears fall before I sniff hard and press the heels of my hands to my eyes.

I need to go for a ride. I jump up and kick off my polka dot shorts, changing into my old ripped jeans with the leather patches everywhere. My riding jeans. I'd never be caught wearing these hideous things off the farm.

Grazing the papered walls with my fingertips, I run down the long hallway that splits our huge house in two. I run through the kitchen. Past Archer, who cocks an eyebrow at me, and jump over Asher's leg as he tries to trip me. Grabbing the keys for the quad off the wall by the phone I stick my feet into my mud-caked boots. I slam through the screen door and jump off the porch onto the dusty path. I hop on my favorite 4-wheel.

"I wouldn't, Graceland." I hear Archer yell, or maybe it was Asher.

"Dad's gunna be pissed," says the other. I can only tell them apart when I'm looking at them. And only because I look at their stupid faces every day.

I ignore them and gun the engine, pressing the gas with my thumb. The wind whips around me as the quad lurches forward, and I squint my eyes into the bright noon sun.

I make it to the end of the driveway in no time and look both ways down the long gravel road that leads to town.

There's nothing but flat field and open road. The tires spit gravel as I steer the quad toward the barns. Standing up, I lift one hand from the handle bars and pull the small elastics that hold my two braids in place and let the wind pull my hair loose. The strands sting as they whip around my head and slap against the skin of my neck, cheeks and shoulders. I love the quad. If only I could drive a real car.

One month and I can get my license. One month and I can have my own freedom. Only one problem. I don't know how to drive. I don't have a car anymore.

Okay, two problems.

I shake my head wildly as I speed down the empty dirt road. I scream as loud as I can, because I can. My favorite part about living on the farm is the space. I'm a mile out and still on our land, only halfway to the stables. The sky is pure blue, stretched out to the horizon in every direction. The wind is warm against my skin. I slow down and turn onto the long path that leads to the stable and to my horse, Belle. It's a totally stupid name but I got her when I was nine and watched Beauty and the Beast like three times a day.

I stop the quad and hop off, cutting the engine but leaving the keys. My cowboy boots, which I only wear riding or working, kick the dry, sun-baked earth up all around me as I make my way to the side of the cracked red barn.

I round the corner expecting Belle but I'm greeted by...

Abs?

Thick, corded, perfectly defined man-abs. I stop and so does my heart. I have to swallow hard to keep it from popping right out of my mouth.

I'm not sure what kind of face belongs to these abs. Whoever's standing in front of me is wiping his forehead with the bottom of a dirty white shirt.

I clear my throat and the guy jumps, dropping his shirt and staring at me with ice blue eyes under thick dark eyebrows. His wild black hair is tangled around his face and soaked in sweat. His lips are thick, angular, and pressed together to match his frown. He kind of looks like Black Beauty, but with insanely blue eyes.

Why am I comparing this guy to a horse? Because he's beautiful and sleek and glistening...and grinning.

I realize I'm staring and narrow my eyes. I never gawk.

"Who are you?" I ask, crossing my arms in front of my tattered plaid button up. Suddenly I'm wishing I was in my little blue sun-dress and wedge heels that make me look thinner, and taller.

And older.

Ice Eyes scans me slowly and it makes me jittery. I'm used to this reaction from guys. Just not in this outfit. I tighten my crossed arms and shift my weight from one foot to the other, digging my boot heel into the cracked earth.

"I might ask you the same thing?" His voice is deep and makes my ankles wobble. He's not my age. No guy in my school looks like this.

But he can't be *too* much older.

"Graceland Holloway. This is my father's farm." I cringe as my country accent comes out as clear as a ringing bell in an empty church.

I bite my lip and Bentley cocks his head to one side. I try so hard to keep the hick side of me hidden, but sometimes it just can't be stopped. This lifestyle, the one Daddy loves so much, was one of the reasons mom left us and I try to keep it locked up. Especially around strangers.

I reach out my hand and Ice Eyes takes a step toward me. I probably shouldn't be shaking strangers' hands without my brothers, or Daddy, around. But this guy is hot and I want a reason to touch him and see if he feels the way I think he does.

"Bentley McKinna." He shakes my hand. Hard and calloused. He's a working guy. The best kind.

"Like the car?" I feel stupid for saying it, but Bentley laughs. His teeth are white as fresh milk.

"Never heard that one before." He's mocking me.

He is like the car. Hard and smooth and sexy...

Seriously, Graceland.

I'm staring again.

I clear my throat and run my hand through my hair, messing it up and tossing it to the side. At school, the hair toss gets me pretty much whatever I want. I don't know why guys like long hair so much, but whatever. If it works...

"So why are you hangin' out in my stable?" I smile my best smile and jut my hip out, forgetting I'm wearing mom jeans.

"I hiked out here." He shrugs.

"Why? It's like 25 miles to town."

"Because I'm supposed to start work for your father tomorrow. Just wanted to see some of the countryside."

I'm about to ask why, because everything looks the same around here. Stand in one spot and turn in a circle. Everything is seen. But I don't get a chance to say anything.

Bentley turns and moves back around the barn. He returns with a duffel over his shoulder. He looks like one of those guys in World War Two movies who are *always* dirty but still manage to be gorgeous.

And this gorgeous hitchhiker is going to be living in my backyard for the summer.

Maybe this summer won't be as bad as I thought.

"I can give you a ride to the house." I point at the quad and Bentley looks around me.

"My bag?"

"Sit on it."

I hope he's watching as I turn and swing my hips on my way back to the quad. If Hunter were here, he'd slap my head and tell me I'm insinuating things far beyond my age and experience. I don't even know what that means. But he says it a lot.

All I know is Bentley's smokin' and I want to have fun with him. No harm in that.

I look back at him, throwing my hair over my shoulder again.

"Are you coming?"

He has a smirk on his face but his eyebrows are pulled low over his crystal eyes. He's thinking.

"How about I drive?" He tosses his bag on the back.

I laugh.

"How 'bout you just get on?"

He climbs behind me and leans back, holding the rack. I take one more quick look over my shoulder at him and gun the engine.

I stand up out of habit, but I know my butt is right at his eye level.

Insinuate my ass.

Born in the Canadian prairies, Allie Brennan enjoyed growing up on a dusty farm but the call of the wild took her up to the snowy mountains of the North where she now resides with her partner and her puppy. Tight Knit is Brennan's debut novel.

Made in the USA
Charleston, SC
03 January 2013